WRIGHT MORRIS

WAR
GAMES

1972

BLACK SPARROW PRESS

LOS ANGELES

SBN 87685-108-1 (paper)
SBN 87685-109-X (signed cloth)

BLACK SPARROW PRESS
P.O. BOX 25603
LOS ANGELES, CALIFORNIA 90025

WAR GAMES

This novel was written during the winter-spring of 1951-52 and was never submitted for publication. Themes and characters that first appear in *War Games* reappear in *The Field Of Vision* and *Ceremony In Lone Tree.*

Wright Morris
Princeton
September, 1971

I

In his fifty-third year a chemical blast burned the beard from the Colonel's face, and gave to his eyes their characteristic powdery blue. Some time later his bushy eyebrows came in white. Silvery streaks of the same color appeared in his hair. To his habitually bored expression these touches gave a certain distinction, a man-of-the-world air, that his barber turned to the advantage of his face. The thinning hair was parted, the lock of silver was deftly curled. The Colonel had an absent-minded way of stroking it back. As he was self-conscious, rather than vain, there was something attractive about this gesture, and a great pity that women didn't seem to interest him. He had married one to reassure himself on that point.

When not away at war the Colonel lived with his wife in an apartment on the Heights, in Brooklyn. She lived at the front with her canary, Jenny Lind, and he lived at the back with his two cats. His wife did not care for cats, particularly, but she had learned to accept the situation, just as the cats had learned, when the Colonel was absent, to shift for themselves. The cleaning women, as a rule, were tipped liberally to be attentive to them. The Colonel supplied the cats with an artificial tree, which they could climb, claw, or puzzle over, and a weekly supply of fresh catnip mice. The mice were given to the cats every Thursday, as on Friday the cleaning woman, with a broom and the vacuum, would try to get the shredded catnip out of the rug. They would then settle back and wait patiently for Thursday again.

The blast improved the Colonel's looks, but it had not been so good for his eyes. They watered a good deal, the pupils were apt to dilate in a strange manner, and he became extremely sensitive to light. In the sun he didn't see any too well. To protect his eyes from the light he wore a large pair of military glasses, with dark lenses, and something like blinders at the sides. He was wearing these glasses when he stepped from the curbing, in uptown Manhattan, and was hit by a pie truck headed south. He was put in the back, with the pies, and carted to a hospital.

He hovered between life and death for several weeks. Nor was there any explanation as to why he pulled through. He had nothing to live for, and his health was not good. In the metal locker at the foot of the bed was the uniform in which he had been delivered, broken up, as the doctor remarked, like a sack of crushed ice. The uniform, however, had come through rather well. There were a few stains, but no bad tears or rips. It had been carefully cleaned, and now hung in the closet waiting for him.

The Colonel, however, showed very little interest in getting up. He seemed to like it, as his wife remarked, well enough in bed. When he coughed, a blue vein would crawl from his hair and divide his forehead, and the salty tears brimming in his weak eyes would stream down his face. He had aged, he was not really alive, but he refused to die. After several weeks he was therefore removed from the ward of hopeless cases, and put among those who were said to have a fifty-fifty chance. Visitors came to this room, and there were radios. From his bed there was a fine view of the city including the East river, the Brooklyn Bridge, part of lower Manhattan, and the harbor from which the Colonel had never sailed. With his military glasses he could see the apartment where his wife and cats lived. On the roofs of the tenements that sprawled below there daily appeared, like a plague of Martian insects, the television aerials that brought to the poor the empty lives of the rich. The Colonel ordered a set, but was told that his failing eyes were too weak.

On the table at his side were a glass of water, boxes of vitamin capsules and pills, an expensive silver lighter, and a blurred photograph of his cats. A bedpan and a carton of cigarettes were on the shelf beneath. The Colonel had a taste for expensive cigarettes, in vacuum tins or flats of fifty, but his pleasure seemed to be in the lighter, which required no flint. The small gas cartridge would light, it was said, many thousand cigarettes. As it made no sound, the Colonel played with it at night. During the day he lit many cigarettes and let them smoke in the room, like incense, but during the night he experimented with the small wiry hairs on his chest. Several twisted together, and ignited, would give off a crackling sound. It pleased him to singe the blonde hairs on his fingers, hold them to his nose. When not playing with the lighter the Colonel slept, or sat for hours with an air of brooding, or used his army glasses to examine the teeming life in the streets. What he saw, however, was no surprise to him. To an old army man it was just another bloody battlefield.

In his fifty-third year, having time on his hands, the Colonel was able to see through the glasses what he had known, so to speak, all his life. Life, to put it simply, was a battleground. Every living thing, great or small, spilled its blood on it. Every day he read the uproar made in the press about the horrors of war, the fear of the draft, and what it would do to the lives of the fresh eighteen-year-olds. Every moment he could see a life more horrible in the streets. Dangers more unjust, risks more uncalculated, and barracks that were more intolerable. Children fell from windows, were struck by cars in the street, were waylaid and corrupted by evil old men, or through some private evil crawled off to corrupt themselves. Loose boards rose up and struck idle women, knives cut their fingers, fire burned their clothes, or in some useless quarrel they suffered a heart attack. The ambulance appeared after every holiday. The sirens moaned through the streets, like spectres, every night. Doors closed on small fingers, windows fell, small dogs bit bigger dogs, or friends and neighbors, and in the full light of day a man would tumble, head first, down the steps to the street. If this man was a neighbor they might pick him up, but if a stranger they would pass him by, walking in an arc around him the way children swing wide of a haunted house. Or they would stand in a circle, blocking the walk, until the man who was paid to touch a dead man felt the wrist for the pulse, or held the pocket mirror to the face. As if the dead man, poor devil, wanted a final look at himself.

All of this struck the Colonel, an old soldier, as a new kind of battleground. "That's life for you," the doctor would say, when the Colonel would trouble to point out that the only safe

9

place for a man, or a soldier, was in bed. Trapped there, so to speak, and unable to get up and put on his pants. For it was with his pants that a man put on the world. He became a part of it, he accepted the risks and the foolishness. The Colonel could see this very clearly in the casualties brought to the ward, the men who had fallen on this nameless battlefield. They lay staring at the same world that seemed to terrify the Colonel, but not one of these men was at all disturbed by it. Everything they saw seemed to appeal to them. Every woman reminded them of their wives, and every child of their own children, and the happy times, the wonderful life they seemed to think they had lived. When another victim appeared in the ward they would cry out to ask him "How are things going?" although it was clear things were still going murderously. That it was worth a man's life to put on his pants and appear in the streets. But not one of these men, broken and battered as they were, by the world they had left, had any other thought but a craving to get back to it. To be broken, battered, and bruised all over again. The Colonel found it hard to believe his eyes—both inside and outside of the window—as the world of men seemed to be incomprehensible. It affected, as he knew it would, his feeble will to live. He did not die, but neither did he live, as if the world both inside and outside of the window was a kind of purgatory, a foretaste of hell but with no possibility of heaven. Once a week his wife, a small attractive woman who referred to him as Mr. Army, brought him cookies made with black-strap molasses, pure brewer's yeast, and wheat germ flour. The recipe was her own, but they were made by the cleaning woman. As Mrs. Foss was several years older than the Colonel, and look-ed from eight to ten years younger, there was no need to argue the importance of blackstrap and brewer's yeast. The Colonel would ask how the cats were doing, read the mail she had brought him, and when she had left he would distribute the cookies in the ward. A young man named Hyman Kopfman was fond of them.

Hyman Kopfman was a small, rabbit-faced little man who belonged in the hopeless ward, but it had been overcrowded and he couldn't afford a room of his own. When he appeared in the ward he had one leg and two arms, but before the first month had ended they had balanced him up, as he put it himself. He stored the cookies away in the sleeve of the gown that he wore pinned up. Something in Hyman Kopfman's blood couldn't live with the rest of Hyman Kopfman, and he referred to this thing as America. Raising the stump of his leg he would say, "Now you're seeing America first!" Then he would laugh. He seemed to get a great kick out of it. Largely because of Hyman Kopfman, there were men in the ward, some of them pretty battered, who looked on the world outside as a happy place. Only the Colonel seemed to see the connection, so to speak. He didn't know what Hyman Kopfman had in his blood, or where it would show up next, but he knew that he had picked it up, like they all did, there in the streets. What Hyman Kopfman knew was that the world was killing him.

Hyman Kopfman was in pain a good deal of the time and sat leaning forward, his small head in his hand, like a man who was contemplating a crystal globe. During the night he often rocked back and forth, creaking the springs. While the Colonel sat playing with his lighter, Hyman Kopfman would talk, as if to himself, but he seemed to be aware that the Colonel was listening. Hyman Kopfman's way of passing the time was not to look at the world through a pair of field glasses, but to turn his gaze, so to speak, upon himself. Then to describe in considerable detail what he saw. As the Colonel was a reserved, reticent man who considered his life and experience private, Hyman Kopfman was something of a novelty. He spoke of himself as if he were somebody else. There were even times when the Colonel thought he was. At the start Hyman Kopfman gave the impression that he would describe everything that had happened; which he did, perhaps, but all that had happened had not added up to much. He was apt to repeat certain things time and time again. There were nights when the Colonel had the impression that he went over the same material the way a wine press went over the pulp of grapes. But there was always something that refused to squeeze out. That, anyhow, was the Colonel's impression, since it was otherwise hard to explain why he went over the same material time and again; here and there adding a touch, or taking one away.

Hyman Kopfman had been born in Vienna—that was what he said. That should have been of some interest in itself, and as the Colonel had never been to Vienna, he always listened in the hope that he might learn something. But Hyman Kopfman merely talked about himself. He might as well have been born in the Bronx, or anywhere else. He had been a frail boy with girlish wrists and pale blue hands, as he said himself, but with something hard to explain that made him likeable. His father had it, but only his mother knew what it was. Hopelessness. It was this, he said, that made him lovable.

The Colonel got awfully tired of this part of the story since Hyman Kopfman was hopeless enough. Too hopeless, in fact. There was nothing about him that was lovable. It was one of the curious conceits he had. His skin was a pale doughy color, and his general health was so poor that when he smiled his waxy gums began to bleed. Thin streaks of red, like veins in marble, showed on his chalky teeth. His eyes were very large, nearly goat-like, with curiously transparent lids, as if the skin had been stretched very thin to cover them. There were times when the eyes, with their large wet whites and peculiarly dilated pupils, gazed upon the Colonel with a somewhat luminous quality. It was disturbing, and had to do, very likely, with his poor health. It was because of his eyes, the Colonel decided, that Hyman Kopfman had picked up the notion that there was something appealing about his hopelessness. Some woman, perhaps his mother, had told him that.

At a very early age Hyman Kopfman had been brought to America. With him came his three brothers, his mother, Frau Tabori-Kopfman, and the room full of furniture that his father had left to them. They went to live in Chicago, where his Uncle Tabori, his mother's brother, had rented an apartment. This apartment was four flights up from the street with a room at the back for Uncle Tabori, a room at the front, called a parlor, and a room in which they lived. In the parlor there were large bay windows but the curtains were kept closed as the light and the circulating air would fade the furniture. It would belong to Paul, the elder brother, when he married someone. In the room were chests full of clothes that his mother had stopped wearing, and his father, a gentleman, had never worn out. They were still as good as new. So it was up to the children to wear them out. It so happened that Mandel Kopfman, the father, had been comparatively small in stature, and his fine clothes would fit Hyman Kopfman, but nobody else. So it was that Hyman Kopfman was accustomed to wear, as he walked between the bedroom and the

12

bathroom, pants of very good cloth, and on his feet the best grade of spats. French braces held up his pants, and there was also a silver-headed cane, with a sword in the handle, that he sometimes carried as he swaggered down the hall. He didn't trouble, of course, to go down the four flights to the street. Different clothes were being worn down there, small tough boys cursed and shouted, and once down, Hyman Kopfman would have to walk back up. He simply couldn't. He never had the strength.

His older brother, Otto, went down all the time as he worked down there, in a grocery, and returned to tell them what it was all about. He also went to movies, and told them about that. At that time his brother Paul had been too shy to go down to the street and work there, so he made the beds and helped his mother around the house. He cooked, he learned to sew, and as he couldn't wear the clothes of Mandel Kopfman, he wore some of the skirts and blouses of his mother, as they fit him all right. It didn't matter, as he never left the rooms. No one but Uncle Tabori ever sat down and talked with them. He worked in the railroad yards that could be seen, on certain clear days, from the roof of the building, where Frau Kopfman went to dry her hair and hang out their clothes. From this roof Hyman Kopfman could see a great park, such as they had at home in Vienna, and in the winter he could hear the ore boats honking on the lake. In spring he could hear the ice cracking up.

Was that Hyman Kopfman's story? If it was, it didn't add up to much. Nor did it seem to gain in the lengthy retelling, night after night. The facts were always the same: Hyman Kopfman had been born, without much reason, in Vienna, and in Chicago he had taken to wearing his father's fancy clothes. As his father had been something of a dandy Hyman Kopfman wore jackets with black satin lapels, shirts with celluloid cuffs and collars, pearl gray spats, French braces, and patent leather shoes. Not that it mattered, since he never went down to the street. He spent day and night in the apartment where he walked from room to room, or with the silver-headed cane he might step into the hall. Concealed in the shaft of the cane was a sword, and when he stepped into the dim gaslit hallway, Hyman Kopfman would draw out the sword and fence the dancing shadow of himself.

Ha! the Colonel would say, being an old swordsman, but Hyman Kopfman had shot his bolt. He could do no more than wag his feeble wrist in the air. His gums would bleed, his goat-like eyes would glow in a disturbing manner, but it was clear that even fencing his shadow had been too much for him. Nothing had really happened. The Colonel doubted that anything ever would.

And then one day—one day just in passing—Hyman Kopfman raised his small head from his hand and said that the one thing he missed, really missed, that is, was the daily walk in the blind garden.

In the what? the Colonel said, as he thought he had missed the word.

In the blind garden, Hyman Kopfman replied. Had he somehow overlooked that? Hadn't he told the Colonel about the blind garden?

The Colonel, a cigarette in his mouth, had wagged his head.

At the back of the building there had been a small walled garden, Hyman Kopfman went on, a garden with gravel paths, shady trees, and places to sit. Men and women who were blind came there to walk. There were also flowers to smell, but they couldn't see them of course.

Well, well—the Colonel had replied, as he thought he now had the key to the story. One of the Kopfmans was blind, and Hyman Kopfman was ashamed to mention it. What difference did it make what Hyman Kopfman wore if his brother Paul, for instance, couldn't see him, and if Paul was blind he would hardly care how he looked himself. What difference did it make if he wore his mother's skirts around the house?

Your brother Paul was blind then—? the Colonel said.

Blind? said Hyman Kopfman, and blinked his own big eyes. Who said Paul was blind?

You were just saying—the Colonel replied.

From the window—interrupted Hyman Kopfman—what he saw below was a tiny private park. There were trees along the path, benches in the shade where the blind could sit. The only thing you might notice was how quiet and peaceful it was. Nobody laughed. The loud voices of children were never heard. It was the absence of children that struck Hyman Kopfman, as he was then very young himself, and liked to think of a park like that as a place for children to play. But the one below the window was not for bouncing balls, nor rolling hoops. No one came to this

14

park to fly a kite, or to skip rope at the edge of the gravel, or to play a game of hide and seek around the trees. In fact there was no need, in a park like that, to hide from anyone. You could be there, right out in the open, and remain unseen. It was Paul Kopfman who pointed out that they might as well go down and sit there, as nobody would know whether they were blind or not. Nobody would notice that Hyman Kopfman was wearing celluloid cuffs and pearl gray spats, or that Paul Kopfman was wearing a skirt and a peasant blouse. Nobody would care, down there, if their clothes were out of date, or that when Hyman Kopfman talked his wax-colored gums were inclined to bleed. It was the talking that made him excited, and the excitement that made his gums bleed, but down there in the garden he was not excited, and nobody cared. There were always flowers, because nobody picked them. There were birds and butterflies, because nobody killed them. There were no small boys with rocks and sticks, nor big boys with guns. There was only peace, and his brother Paul sat on the wooden benches talking with the women, as he didn't seem to care how old, and strange, and ugly they were. In some respects, he might as well have been blind himself.

How long did this go on—? the Colonel said, as he knew it couldn't go on forever. Nothing out of this world, nothing pleasant like that, ever did.

Well, one day his brother Otto—Hyman Kopfman said—his brother Otto put his head out the window and . . .

Never mind—! said the Colonel, and leaned forward as if to shut him up. He wagged his hand at the wrist, and the blue vein on his forehead crawled from his hair.

A man like you, Hyman Kopfman said, an old soldier, a Colonel, a man with gold medals—

Never mind! the Colonel had said, and took from the table his silver lighter, holding it like a weapon, his arm half cocked, as if ready to throw.

Was Hyman Kopfman impressed? Well, he just sat there: he didn't go on. He smiled, but he didn't repeat what Otto had said. No, he just smiled with his bleeding gums, then raised the pale blue stump of his leg, sighted down the shinbone, pulled the trigger, and sang *Bang!* He was like that. He didn't seem to know how hopeless he was.

For example, this Kopfman had only one foot but he sent out

15

both of his shoes to be polished: he had only one arm, but he paid to have both sleeves carefully pressed. The metal locker at the foot of his bed contained the pin stripe suit with the two pair of pants, one pair with left leg neatly folded, and pinned to the hip. Some people might ask if a man like that needed two pair of pants. It was strange behavior for a person who was dying day by day. Not that he wanted very much, really—no, hardly more than most people had—all he really seemed to want was the useless sort of life that the Colonel had lived. To have slept with a woman, to have fought in a war, to have won or lost a large or small fortune, and to have memories, before he died, to look back to. Somehow, Hyman Kopfman had picked up the notion that life was hardly worth living, but it was no consolation, since he had lived so little of it. He had picked up the facts, so to speak, without having had the fun. He always used the word "fun" as he seemed to think that was what the Colonel had had.

Night after night the Colonel listened to this as he played with his lighter, or smoked too much, but he said very little as he felt that Hyman Kopfman was very young. Not in years, perhaps, but in terms of the experience he should have had. His idea of fun was not very complicated. His idea of life being what it was, the Colonel found it hard to understand why he hadn't reached out and put his hands on it. But he hadn't. Perhaps this thing had always been in his blood. Or perhaps life in America had not panned out as he had thought. At the first mention of Chicago, Hyman Kopfman would wave his stubby arm toward the window, roll his eyes, and make a dry rattle in his throat. That was what he felt, what he seemed to think, about America. But there was nothing that he wanted so much as to be out there living in it.

The case of Hyman Kopfman was indeed strange, but not so strange, in some respects, as the case of the older man in the bed on his right. The Colonel had been failing; now for no apparent reason he began to improve. Now that Hyman Kopfman was there beside him—a hopeless case if there ever was one—the Colonel's pulse grew stronger, he began to eat his food. He sat propped up in bed in the manner of a man who would soon be up. He even gazed through the window like a man who would soon be out. Here you had the Colonel, who had nothing to live for, but nevertheless was getting better, while Hyman Kopfman, who hungered for life, was getting worse. It didn't make sense, but

16

that was how it was. Not wanting to live, apparently, was still not wanting to die. So the Colonel, day by day, seemed to get better in spite of himself.

The very week that Hyman Kopfman took a turn for the worse, the Colonel took that turn for the better that led the doctor to suggest that he ought to get up and walk around. Adjust himself, like a new-born babe, to his wobbly legs. So he was pushed out of the bed, and the terry cloth robe that hung for months, unused, in the closet, was draped around his sloping shoulders and a pair of slippers were put on his feet. In this manner he walked the floor from bed to bed. That is to say he toddled, from rail to rail, and the effort made the sweat stand on his forehead and the blue vein crawl like a slug from his thinning hair. But everybody in the ward stared at him enviously. He could feel in their gaze the hope that he would trip, or have a relapse. But at least they were courteous on the surface, they remarked how much stronger he was looking, and made flattering comments on how well he carried himself. They spoke of how fine he would soon look in his uniform. All this from perfect strangers; but Hyman Kopfman, the one who had spoken to him intimately, snickered openly and never tired of making slurring remarks. He referred to the Colonel's soft arms as chicken wings. He called attention to the unusual length of the Colonel's neck. Naturally, the accident that had nearly killed the Colonel had not widened his shoulders any, and there was some truth in the statement that he was neck from the waist up. Nor had the Colonel's wide bottom, like that of a pear, which seemed to hold his figure upright, escaped Hyman Kopfman's critical eye. Nor his feet, which were certainly flat for any army man. A less disillusioned man than the Colonel would have made an official complaint, or brought up the subject of Hyman Kopfman's two-pants suit. But he said nothing. He preferred to take it in his stride. One might even say that he seemed to wax stronger on it. It was this observation, among others, that upset Hyman Kopfman the most, and led him to say things of which he was later ashamed. It was simply too much, for a dying man, to see one getting well who had nothing to live for, and this spectacle always put him into a rage. It also considerably hastened his end. It became a contest, of sorts, as to whether the Colonel would get back on his feet before Hyman Kopfman lost another limb, or managed to die. In this

17

curious battle, however, Hyman Kopfman's will power showed to a great advantage, and he deteriorated faster than the Colonel managed to improve. He managed to die, quite decently in fact, during the night. A Saturday night, as it happened, and the Colonel was able to call his wife and ask her to send a suitable floral offering.

2

Hyman Kopfman died on a Saturday night, and on Sunday the Colonel, in his terry cloth robe, sat in the sunlight of the window watching the nurse make up the new bed. She was of the Colonel's age, but not especially communicaitve. She had seen them—as she liked to say—come and go. She smoothed the sheets with a disinterested hand, as a maid would finish a bed in a hotel room, then took Hyman Kopfman's "effects" from the metal locker at the foot of the bed. The suit had been removed for the services. There remained, however, a blue serge coat and two pairs of pants. There was also a pair of well shined shoes, one worn at the heel, one practically new, and the cheap black fiber bag that had been brought into the room by the taxi man. It contained nothing. It had been part of Hyman Kopfman's front. The Colonel tried to imagine what kind of man would want to put up a front of that sort, but he did not know much about people like that. The army, perhaps, had cut him off from certain things. As he watched the nurse put the shoes in the bag, the heel that was worn, the sole that wasn't, it occurred to the Colonel that not a person had visited him. No letters had come to Hyman Kopfman —none had been sent off. Every day he had talked about his people, but what sort of people were they to let a boy like Hyman Kopfman die like that? Were they dead? Or had he just lost track of them. He had talked of Chicago, but that had been many years ago.

"What about his people—?" the Colonel said, as Mrs. Lynch stood there before him. She was folding, in a professional manner, a pair of his pants.

"What about them?" Mrs. Lynch said, as she had seen enough of people.

"Have they," the Colonel said, "been notified?" Leaning over the bag, Mrs. Lynch nodded her head. "They live near by?" Mrs. Lynch nodded again.

"It just crossed my mind," the Colonel said, "that in six weeks time no one came to see him. I suppose they knew?"

"I suppose they did," Mrs. Lynch said.

Eyeing the cheap bag, the Colonel said, "Where did Mr. Kopfman live?"

"All I know is that the bag goes to The Regent Arms." Mrs. Lynch closed the bag with a snap, and stepped back to look at it.

"*The* Regent Arms?" This residential hotel, one of the most expensive, was just a block down the street from where he lived.

"I suppose there's only one." Mrs. Lynch pressed her mouth into a thin line.

"The Regent Arms is a very fine place." The Colonel had another look at the black fiber bag. It was not even fiber. Just pressed black paper with a coat of shellac.

"I've often noticed," Mrs. Lynch said, folding her arms to make a pronouncement, "that the people with money are not the ones to throw it away. That's why they have it." She gave the Colonel a look that implied she meant a good deal more than she was saying. He got it, and replied—"Well, I suppose you're right."

"I know I'm right." Mrs. Lynch picked up the bag, started off with it.

"I was just thinking—" the Colonel said, and Mrs. Lynch knew that he had been. With the bag, she came back to the foot of his bed. "The Regent Arms is right on my way, and if it would save you any trouble—"

"It wouldn't save me any," said Mrs. Lynch, "but I suppose it would save somebody."

"I got to know him pretty well, don't think his people got around much. Just crossed my mind that his people, his mother might be sick. It might be quite a little trip for her to make."

"If it's his mother," Mrs. Lynch said, "she's married again,

20

as her name is Tabori. Mrs. Tabori is the name we have."

"It's probably someone related," the Colonel replied.

"It's entirely up to you," Mrs. Lynch said, "if you want to take the trouble you're certainly welcome. If they don't call for it, you're certainly welcome to it." She started off again, then she turned. "Colonel Foss, are you really leaving?"

It took the Colonel a moment to nod his head. Something like that might set him back a week or two. He closed his eyes for a moment. "Mrs. Lynch, would you check on The Regent Arms? If there's more than one I—" Mrs. Lynch cut him off.

"I'll check it," she said, and went off with Hyman Kopfman's bag and the sheets from his bed under her arm.

On Friday, the first day of spring, from the telephone booth at the end of the hallway, the Colonel called his wife. She was there. She said it was good to hear his voice. He said he was up now, and dressed, and looking down at his watch he went on to say that he ought to be home within an hour or so. Was there anything she would like him to pick up? When he was in Manhattan, or at the Club, the Colonel always made it a point to call his wife as there might be something at the delicatessen that he could pick up. But there was nothing. She would be there waiting for him. Whenever he called her his wife always said that she would be there, waiting for him, and it always pleased the Colonel, though of course it didn't mean much of anything. It simply meant that she would be there to buzz the door. He would not have to put down whatever he was carrying and use his own keys. Still, it pleased him to know that she would be there, and now he went on to say that he might be delayed, five minutes or so, as he had a parcel of Hyman Kopfman's to drop off. He had been the young man who liked her cookies so much. When he spoke of cookies his wife remembered that they might need a loaf of Pepperidge bread, as now that he was home they would be eating more of it. The Colonel said he would take care of that, and then she hung up.

Although wobbly on his pins, as Hyman Kopfman had said, the Colonel was a hard man to judge once he had been buttoned and strapped into his uniform. He had the bearing, which is to say that though his knees were like the legs of folding chairs, his

21

sense of insecurity showed a bit in his walk, but not in his face. The waver might strike the stranger as a matter of style. He walked—just to get the air, and the feel of a stretch of pavement —from the hospital entrance to the corner of Park Avenue. There he took a cab, not because he was tired, or because of the weight of the parcel he carried, but because the black fiber bag had led several people to turn for a second look at him. One of the loose shoes made a rattling sound as he walked along.

The Colonel told the driver to take his time, and out on the bridge over the East river he leaned forward in the cab to get a better view of Brooklyn Heights. He could see that the French doors at the back of his apartment were closed. In a month or so, with the warm weather, he would open them. The cats spent the morning and the evening on the balcony. At the thought of the cats the Colonel made a sound as if clearing his throat before spitting, and which was intended to resemble a sound the cats made themselves. Hearing it, they would leave the balcony and come to him.

Thinking of the cats made the Colonel smile, and one might have thought that the view of the river, or the beetle shaped ferries crossing the bay, had touched a sentimental part of an old soldier's heart. The view from the bridge, including as it did so much of the war, and so much of the peace, was a proper subject for a show of sentimentality. The wind up the river had led the Colonel to blink his watery eyes. Everything that he saw was unchanged, familiar—after all, he had been gazing at it for months —but now that he was back, within it, something struck him as strange. It was not, that is, as he had left it. No, not quite. Perhaps the long idleness had given a fanciful turn to his mind. When he stepped from the cab, the lightness of the bag he carried brought a sly smile to his face. The pants were light, as they had never really been filled. The coat was light, as one sleeve had seldom been used. There was nothing curious about such a notion except that a man like the Colonel should have it—it seemed to indicate that he was still somewhat out of this world.

Sometime before the war—the last war—the Colonel was in the habit of taking his wife to the roof garden of The Regent Arms. In the summer it was cool, the music was pleasant, and as a rule there was a class of people who could appreciate a woman like his wife. The Colonel liked to sit facing the river, with the music at his back, and gaze at the windows that were still lit up in the skyscrapers. In some magazine he had come across the statement that at night office buildings were the brothels of the business world, and that summer this statement, for some puzzling reason, preyed on his mind. Nearly all of the things that he had taken for granted, such as office buildings, women, and work after hours, suddenly took on a special and sinister significance. Objects like desks and water coolers, words like PRIVATE OFFICE (always to be seen on frosted glass windows), transported the Colonel to a highly charged world of illicit love. The mention of the words *My Boss*, or *Secretary*, might make him blush. And it had been getting worse, rather than better, right up to the evening when Mrs. Foss, searching in her bag for the keys to the apartment, dropped one of The Regent Arms demitasse spoons on the loud tile floor. The Colonel had been a man more than forty years of age, but it had been quite a shock.

At that time The Regent Arms had been one of those places well known for its linen and fine silver service, a luxury they gave up, understandably, during the war. Before they gave it up Mrs. Foss had acquired thirty-seven of the spoons. If his wife had been a small town girl from Terre Haute—in town for the week, and then headed back there—the Colonel would not have found it difficult to understand. That is to say, he knew that kind of impulse himself. He had several bath towels from a fine hotel in Los Angeles. But his wife had lived for years just a block down the street, and the light from the enormous blinking sign on the roof made a glow on the walls of their rooms all night long. It was out of the question that such spoons would ever be used. Each spoon bore the stamp of the familiar coat of arms. It had been a blow that set the Colonel back farther than the one he had received from the truck full of pies. That could be explained; with a pencil and paper he could figure it out. But for no sensible reason, just to have them (to *have* them, that is, for *nothing*) a cultivated woman like his wife had swiped thirty-seven demi-tasse spoons and kept them in the box that his military brushes had come in. In *his* drawer. Under *his* shirts and socks. When the spoon had dropped out on the floor, she had said, "I'm just glad I started when I did. Did you see that woman stealing forks—forks, imagine—at the table near the door?" That had been all. That had been all from Mrs. Claudine Foss, his wife.

Although he had stolen nothing himself, the Colonel could never enter The Regent Arms without activating a complex sense of guilt. On the roof his wife had made away with many spoons, and he himself had had questionable thoughts. Now he had the cheap black bag in his hand, and as he crossed the spacious lobby to the desk he was aware that the clerk had an eye on him.

"I would like to leave a parcel," the Colonel said, avoiding a more definite description, "for a Mrs. Kopfman."

"A Mrs. Kopfman? Are you sure the name is Kopfman?"

"Excuse me," said the Colonel, "the name is Mrs. Tabori. Kopfman is the name of the deceased."

"You ring?" said a voice. The clerk had not rung, but a jockey-sized bellhop, with the face of an aging child, was there at the Colonel's elbow. "Somebody ring?" he repeated.

The clerk ignored him.

"I have a parcel for a Mrs. Tabori," said the Colonel.

"Would it be a Mr. and Mrs. Tabori?" The bellhop's red hat, tilted on his head, gave him the look of an organ grinder's monkey. "Mrs. Tabori is my wife," the bellhop said.

It was not unusual for the Colonel to feel that he was playing some role in an amateur production. The dialogue would have that theatrical falseness. If silent, he expected to hear the voice of a prompter in the wings.

"You wish to see Mrs. Tabori?" the bellhop asked.

"I was asked to leave a parcel," the Colonel countered. The bellhop thrust his small head forward for a look at it. The Colonel left his hand on the case in such a manner the bellhop did not disturb it. "Is Mrs. Tabori available?"

The bellhop paused to consider. The Colonel had the impression that he had forgotten his lines. "She's resting," he replied. "I'll see that she gets it."

There was no reason for the Colonel to question his intentions, but ficey little men made the Colonel stubborn.

"I gave Mr. Kopfman my word," he said, "that I would deliver it personally. They are personal effects. I understand that Mr. Kopfman was her son."

"By a former marriage," the bellhop quickly replied. That did not change the Colonel's sense of obligation. Quite the con-

24

trary, he was relieved to think this unpleasant character was *not* his father.

"If you don't mind stepping to the back, Mr.—"

"Foss," said the Colonel. "Colonel Foss."

The bellhop bowed as if greatly honored, the jacket pulling away from his bony neck. "If you'll follow me, sir—" and off he went, the Colonel tagging along with the fiber case. Actually the very lightness of the case was a problem, and might require something of an explanation. Had his mother been informed that he had lost even more than his life? The bellhop led him clear to the rear of the building where the rooms were plainly for employees only, the hall narrow, the doors small, like those on a ship. "She's hard of hearing, you know—" the bellhop said, but of course the Colonel didn't know that. The door opened on a room bathed in a green, watery light. This was due to the plants crowding the windows, as well as the diminished light of the airshaft. The Colonel thought the room empty until he noticed the flickering movement near the window. A woman sewing, or knitting; her head was tipped over her work. Before the bellhop spoke she raised her eyes to the Colonel's face as if he had spoken. It may have been the lambent glow of the light that gave her eyes such luminous depths. The Colonel was something of a student of eyes, being fond of cats. The resemblance to Hyman Kopfman was striking, allowing for the difference in their ages.

"I've brought you your son's things—" said the Colonel, forgetting that she was hard of hearing. Did she follow the gist of it? "AHHhhhhh," she said.

"She just don't hear much," the bellhop said, and shrugged his shoulders at what couldn't be helped. He took the fiber case from the Colonel, and placed it on the floor where she could reach it. "She'll look at it later. She'll get the idea when she looks inside."

The Colonel had rather hoped he could spare her that, but after all, it was none of his business. Any effort on his part to explain would only make matters worse.

"If she has any questions—about Mr. Kopfman . . . "

"I'll explain it to her," said the bellhop.

"AhhhHHHHhhhhh," she said.

The Colonel gathered that this wordless response constituted her conversation. His own face being in the light he smiled, turned back to the door.

"I'll fill her in later," the bellhop added, but he did not lead the Colonel back to the lobby, nor actually thank him for what he had done. The Colonel didn't let this bother him too much, since he was familiar with insolence in *small* people, and the cunning they used to deal with people who were larger. As an old army man he was accustomed to all of that. He returned to the street, pausing on the corner to glance at the windows of his apartment, secure in the knowledge that the curtains concealed his wife. For her benefit he snapped his fingers in the manner of a man who had remembered something, just in time, so that when she asked him what he was doing on the corner, he would say that he had remembered something, and snapped his fingers. The one thing she liked about him was that he wasn't as complicated as he looked.

The year the Colonel met his wife her face sometimes appeared in the scenic background of theatrical productions, or the blurred photographs that on occasion showed up in the newspapers. Even there, however, it was unmistakeable. No matter what the setting, or how dim the lighting, this face stood out. This was not merely the opinion of a lovesick soldier but a fairly commonplace observation, and held true, the Colonel discovered, from every part of the theatre. The more the Colonel tried to puzzle it out the more the alabaster face of Claudine Baker, although actually far in the background, always gave the impression of being at the front of the stage. This same curious characteristic came out in her voice. It was a small voice, oddly flat, but once the Colonel had filtered it out, and knew that this sound came from Miss Baker, he could hear it distinctly above the baying of the leading roles. So could the critics, who were unkind enough to point this out. The Colonel was no judge at all in these matters, but he knew that her voice, whether good or bad, seemed to have the power to come to the front of the stage. Like her face, it refused to blend with the faces of others or the scenic background, and a stranger to the opera might feel that she was the star of the cast, waiting for the moment to be led to the center of the stage. There had been an aura about Claudine Baker, and, as some men had troubled to point out, it proved to be a great pity she could neither sing, dance nor act. When she had grasped that, which took some doing, she had been the one to propose to the Colonel. Nobody would believe that, of course, but how many things of interest did anybody believe?

When Claudine Baker gazed across the table at the man she had selected for a mate, it was never at his eyes, or what at times might be regarded as an expression. She took the larger view, one that is usually seen through the finder of candid cameras, an ensemble type portrait that included head, shoulders, and a portion of the dining table, set up for the meal. Somewhat detached and impersonal. The Colonel strangers saw was the person his wife assumed him to be.

For a man of his temperament this point of view had much to recommend it. The question of who he really was, or who she had married—so often a ticklish point with married couples— never came up. She saw who he was, very clearly, in the glances he received from others, most of them military personnel checking on his rank. Rank was important to the Colonel's wife or she would hardly have bothered with the demi-tasse spoons, each with the heraldic monogrammed emblem of The Regent Arms. They had it, the Colonel had it, and it was no small thing to have in common in an age where distinctions were increasingly hard to make. The Colonel would not soon forget the reply of his wife to a clerk showing her water color sketches: "I'm sure it will grow on you, Madam," he said. "I don't want it to *grow* on me," she replied. "I want to like it right off." The ties that bound them could not have been more succinctly put.

In the vestibule, where the demi-tasse spoon had made such a clatter on the floor, the Colonel pressed the button and then put his ear to the speaking tube. Libby Bird would answer, and say, "Who dat?"

And the Colonel would make a false voice and reply, "Jus us chickens, Boss," and Libby Bird would laugh so hard she might forget to press the buzzer for the door. The Colonel was very fond of Libby Bird, as she not only understood cats, but she laughed at all the stories he brought home for his wife. But it was not her voice he heard in the tube.

"Yes—?" said the Colonel's wife.

27

"Oh, it's me," said the Colonel.

"Do I smell something burning?" said his wife, and the Colonel laughed, Ha-ha-ha, as that was really pretty clever. His wife liked to play little games. She had turned her voice away from the tube, as if she really might smell something burning.

"That all depends—" the Colonel said, glad to find his wife in good humor, but he was not very clever at the game himself. There was no answer, but that might be part of the game. Sometimes she let him stand in the vestibule for quite a little while. She also liked to play games with the cleaning women, but with the exception of Libby Bird, who took, as she said, Missus Foss in her stride, most of them didn't care for Mrs. Foss' innocent fun. Two or three times a month, for example, the Colonel would find at his plate a knife that would bend, or a fork with soft rubber prongs. His wife would laugh until the tears came into her eyes. There was something mechanical but infectious about this laugh. It had led the Colonel to repeatedly fool himself, just to please his wife. One of the things that amused her the most was the fact that he never seemed to learn, which confirmed a theory she had about men. Creatures of habit, was her way of putting it. The cleaning women were not creatures of habit, and after two or three misfires with the knife, and the soft prongs of the fork, they were no longer seen about the house. The Colonel had remarked a troubled sense of wonder in the gaze of some of these women, as they had all been told, of course, that he had *never* really caught on. He was a man, and men were creatures of habit, as she had proved.

The Colonel gave another press to the button, just to remind her that he was still in the vestibule, playing the game. Another game she liked to play—being thirsty made him think of it—had to do with the plastic ice cubes she put in his drinks. She had a dozen or so of these cubes, each one with something unpleasant in it, like a fly, a snail, a rusty nail, or a soiled piece of string. They appeared to be floating in his high-balls all summer long. Something like that would amuse her all evening, and it seemed a small price to pay, in the Colonel's mind, to give her so much innocent fun. The sober side of his wife's nature had to do with diet, birth control, and her relationship with assorted cleaning women. These things were not apt to be humorous. In his wife's opinion, cleaning women were an essential part of the social structure, as

28

they knew, as few people did, how the other half lived. His wife took this responsibility seriously. The *little games* she liked to play with the help were part of it. The Colonel didn't follow this theory too well, but just as his wife felt the need to amuse the cleaning women, he felt the need to amuse his wife. If he could do it with a rubber pronged fork, why he would.

He gave the button another press, then he leaned forward, his mouth to the tube, and said in a firm voice—*Knock, knock, knock.* But there was no reply, and the door did not buzz. In this extremity, the Colonel used his own keys. Either his wife had been called to the phone, which sometimes happened, or the game had moved to the upper level, the apartment front door. Even if open, he would say *knock, knock, knock,* again.

On the third floor landing, where he stopped to rest, the Colonel could see that the door stood open, but there was no sound from his wife's canary, Jenny Lind. Jenny Lind would sing when his wife sang, when she laughed and joked with the cleaning women, or played records on the phonograph. When she did not sing it was not a good sign. In the front room the lights were off, but the Colonel could see the flickering shadows cast by the candles in the dining room. The thought of the candles made his eyes smart. They would be there on the table, just eye level, so that he had to peer around them, but too tall to throw any light on his plate. The Colonel liked to see what he was going to eat. It was part of its taste. But his wife liked the soft glow of candles, and the four months she had spent in England, around a great log fire, had given her a distaste for electric light. She kept a taper, as she called it, burning in her own room during the night.

At the door the Colonel said again, *Knock, knock, knock,* and when there was no answer he put in his head. If she was behind the door, his wife would say Boooo!, but now she said nothing, and the Colonel realized that he was alone in the room. The cloth hood was over the cage of Jenny Lind. As he stood there a draft blew from the back, sputtering the long flames on the candles, and the Colonel remarked that it had a strong, acrid smell. He thought he detected grease, and burned flesh. He was about to call out for Libby, when the kitchen door, creaking in the draft, opened far enough so that he could see the length of the apartment. The kitchen was smoke filled but empty, and far at the back he could see that his wife stood out on the balcony with a smoking pan. She was emptying the contents of the pan into the air. Libby Bird, the cook, was nowhere in sight, and the Colonel observed that his wife was wearing the plastic apron she had given to Libby Bird. He turned quickly—a matter of instinct—and hurried back through the door into the hall. He stood there, quietly, until he heard the water sizzle into the pan. After a moment his wife said, "You'll have to excuse me, Mr. Foss, as I just can't seem to be everywhere at once." That was not like her. That was not like her at all.

"If I'd had any idea—" said the Colonel, then stopped there and added, "Libby's sick?" She often was. Or said she was.

"It really doesn't concern me any longer," said his wife, calmly but firmly, "what she is." The Colonel felt an impulse to step forward and put a soothing hand on his wife's shoulder, but over the years he had learned that this impulse was not right. He stood there. His wife let the water run into the pan. The lobes of her small ears were flushed, and her hair was untidy in a manner that made her even more attractive than usual.

"If I'd only known," the Colonel said, "that Libby—"

"They are all the same," she said, "it's not a bit more than I've expected," and the Colonel thought he detected a note of affection in her voice. She had known it would happen. It had happened as she had known. She was pleased that these people did not disappoint her.

In the field of human relations, as it was narrowed down to assorted cleaning women, the Colonel had early recognized something very original in his wife. Something superior to the general point of view. Fond as he was of Libby Bird, for example, the Colonel would have fired her on the spot the day her breath was scented with his House of Lords gin. Naturally, she lied about it. She lied about everything. When the Colonel took to marking the bottle, Libby Bird sometimes resorted to water, sometimes to rubbing alcohol, to keep the contents level with the mark. This was a personal matter, but his wife saw it impersonally. She did not let Libby Bird obstruct the larger view. The temptation was there, and people like that were not going to resist. The Colonel's wife held out for Libby Bird because she recognized her as *one of those people,* and representative of something much bigger than herself. Another woman would have cursed Libby Bird, personally, when she called up at half past eleven to say that she had *the cramp,* and would not make it. But Claudine Foss kept the larger picture in view. She never let it upset her, personally. When the situation got out of hand, as it seemed to, why she would end it: experience had taught her it was no more than what she had a right to expect.

"Libby is sick?" the Colonel repeated.

"We've dispensed with her services."

The only thought to cross the Colonel's mind was about his cats. Libby Bird had liked cats. They had liked Libby Bird. Through the door he could see one cat on the bed, and beyond the bed, on the balcony, the nervy cat, Jackson, sniffing the burned lamb chop grease. Seeing the cats reminded the Colonel that he was home, in his own place, and among, as it were, his own kind.

"Wouldn't they do it tonight," his wife said, "now wouldn't they do it tonight?"

She meant Libby. Libby as she represented the group. It occurred to the Colonel that the situation was harder on his wife than himself, as more than a mere cleaning woman was letting her down. She was being let down by the group, by the human race itself.

"Why don't we just step out," the Colonel said, "why don't we step out to The Regent Arms?"

His wife turned off the water and stood there, looking at him. With a moist hand she smoothed back her hair. He thought she was turning over in her mind the pros and cons of The Regent Arms, but as usual she was thinking of something else.

"You've lost weight," she said, matter of factly, "haven't you?" Before he could answer she came forward, the pot holder still in her hand, and smoothed down a bulge in his coat. It fit him loosely, and there was too much slack in the belt.

"I guess I have lost some—" he said, and made an effort to widen his shoulders, but his arms, after flapping, drooped limp at his side. In another woman's face he might have seen that he was tired, which was how he felt, but in the face of his wife he saw only that she was still flushed. "Yes, I guess I've lost some," he said, and as his wife picked the lint from his sleeve he felt the breeze off the river cool on his face. It smelled the same. Nothing at all had changed. The cat, Jackson, was still curious, sniffing the air on the balcony, and the white cat, Georgia, was not at all curious, and still on the bed. His wife had come forward to pick

31

the lint from his sleeve. He felt the same impulse to rest his hand, just for a moment, on her shoulder, but he resisted this impulse as he knew what she would say. She would say, very simply, "Mr. Army, your hand is warm." In the summer it was warm, in the winter it was cold. That too was the same, but something had changed, for the Colonel said, apropos of nothing, "You remember Hyman Kopfman?"

"Kopfman—" she said. "Isn't that Jewish?"

The Colonel raised a hand to his face, making a rasping sound on his chin. He needed a shave. "I suppose I ought to shave," he said.

"Why don't I just scramble some eggs?" she said. Turning back to the kitchen, she stopped to straighten one of the smoking candles, as it had tipped. "There's a letter from your mother," she said, pointing at it, and the Colonel let himself down in the chair facing the table, the candles, and the letter on his plate. The stamp was gone, as Libby Bird had soaked it off. She had been fond of stamps, the Colonel remembered, and what she called a lil snifter of gin.

The letter lay on the table unopened during the meal. Since the explosion and his weakened eyes, the Colonel let his wife puzzle out the letters, and the faded yellow clippings, that he periodically received. His mother, a woman of eighty-four, still wrote a firm illegible scrawl on the cheap manila paper with the wide green stripes, like popcorn bags. As a matter of economy she always wrote on both sides of the page. The message not merely reappeared on the back, but was impressed like a carbon on the page beneath, and there were usually holes, neatly drilled, to mark the periods and to dot the i's. He received one of these letters a month before Christmas, reminding him of the things that she really needed, and not to waste his money on trifles and tommyrot for her. If another letter came, during the rest of the year, it was because the Maumee Herald or the Nonpareil had come out with something new on the career of Milton Ashley. The Colonel had been born on the same day (but forty minutes later, as his luck would have it) in the same town, the same year, and just across the tracks from the fine house where Milton Ashley saw the light of day. This had made a lasting impression on

32

his mother's mind. The Ashley family were important local people, *the* local people: they owned the lumber yard, they ran the paper, they saw to it that the town had a park and a bandstand, and, to top it off, they brought Milton Ashley into this world. It was no mere accident, the Colonel's mother was sure, that Roger Foss saw the same light, on the same day as Milton Ashley. Very early, the name of Milton Ashley was coupled with that of the Little Lord Jesus, and produced as a rule the same effect on Roger Foss' mind: a sense of having been born with much too little, much too late. Milton Ashley made the most of a forty minute start. He won the Bibles, he won the races, he captained the teams, he headed the classes, and he coined the phrases that were like pebbles in the Colonel's mouth. And when it was known that Milton Ashley had received an appointment to Annapolis, there had ceased to be a doubt as to where Roger Foss' future would lie. He would go to West Point—where he finally went, after more than two years of wire pulling, and the help of the influential Ashley family, of course.

That should have been enough, an ordinary mother would have let it rest at that point, but Caroline Foss was not an ordinary mother. She read nothing but the Maumee Herald, for example, which gave her a limited view of the world, but a guided tour of the rise of Milton Ashley. As Mrs. Ashley had remained in the town, and never lost contact with her illustrious son, the Maumee Herald was seldom out of touch with him long. Caroline Foss clipped all of these reports from the paper, underlined the salient points with pencil, then sent them on, in carefully pressed batches, to her son. During the war Commander Ashley had distinguished himself in the Far East, where he personally knew MacArthur, Mme. Chiang Kai-shek, and the boy ruler of Tibet. But for all of that he was still, as he said, a Maumee boy. The one place he wanted to be was home. He was never there, of course, as duty called him elsewhere, or he snatched a few moments with his wife and three daughters at their Honolulu home. The Colonel's mother always underlined these observations, as the Colonel had not been home in ten years, and his very brief letters were not strong in nostalgia. The happiest days of his life, as it happened, were the years of the great depression, as even Milton Ashley found the going a little tough. Until the war, very little had been heard from him. But with the war, Milton Ashley, as well as Caroline Foss and the Maumee Herald, took a new lease on life. The rising star of Milton Ashley kept them all looking up.

As the Colonel now complained about his eyes, and found it out of the question to read newspaper clippings, his wife made it a point to read his mother's letters to him. Sometimes his wife would put the letter aside—at a familiar turn of phrase in his mother's description—and gaze at the Colonel, he seemed to feel, for the first time. She saw him, at such times, through his mother's eyes. The Colonel recognized in his wife a point of view so much like his mother's that he knew she might have written these letters herself. She would have underlined the same important things. If she happened to be in a position to see that Colonel Foss was not Commander Ashley, she still felt the need for example and comparison. It was this impersonal kind of vision that made their judgements so superior, as the particular man, or woman, didn't figure very large in it. *Man* was represented by Milton Ashley, just as the general no-account run of people was represented so wonderfully by Libby Bird. These were obvious things, beyond questioning. The skeptical, doubting, insecure male mind that he sometimes felt stirring within him the Colonel recognized as a very expendable thing. In these women he sensed what was durable. It was not vacillating, subject to taste, nor heir to the ills the flesh was heir to; it was not, curiously, either Milton Ashley or Libby Bird. No, it was something more impersonal, and more terrible. Hyman Kopfman, with his flair for strong words, might have called it horrible.

"And from Bangkok—" his wife read, then half turned from the table so that the candlelight fell on the clipping in her hand.

"From Bangkok?" the Colonel replied, to show that he was still listening.

"—comes news that Milton Ashley has just received the Order of the Siam Crown, 4th Class. The pinning on of the decoration—"

The Colonel took from his pocket a cigar, removed the wrapper, the label, and then smoothed the label out, carefully, on his plate. He bent his head over the plate as if to read the label for the first time. At the pause in his wife's reading he said, "Well, well—and how are the kids doing?" as the Ashley children seemed very familiar to him.

"You never did see—" his wife continued, "such travelled

34

young ladies as Wendy, Judy and even little Pamela Ashley. Of course you know that they flew from Rome to Bangkok—" but there she paused again, her head cocked to one side like her canary, Jenny Lind. The cat, Jackson, was pushing his plastic bowl around in the kitchen.

"And from Bangkok—" the Colonel said.

"—back to Rome," continued his wife, "which they all saw upside down and inside out. They had the benefit of a highly recommended female guide. Mrs. Ashley flew from Bangkok to Singapore, as Milton could see that a riot was looming, and there she was isolated in her hotel for nearly five days. Then—" but the cat, Jackson, had got the bowl to rocking, and they sat there, silent, waiting for the wobbling noise to stop.

"I think I'd better go feed him." The Colonel stood up. From the kitchen, the plastic bowl in his hand, the door to the refrigerator open, the Colonel said, "and from Singapore to where—?"

"—to Minneapolis, where, in more than twenty thousand miles of travel, Pamela ran into her first serious delay. She was held up three hours before she could take a plane to Maumee."

The Colonel stood in the kitchen, facing the refrigerator door. At this point he usually interrupted to say that one of these days—one of these days—he would have to get back to Maumee. But now he said nothing, he stood there watching the cats eat. They were very dainty. Sometimes they would make an awful racket *for* their food, then stand there, fussy and prissy, delicately sniffing what he had put down for them. He controlled the impulse to push the nose of Jackson into his plate.

"I see they're still shedding—" the Colonel said, as some of the white cat's fur, a patch of it, had stuck to his pants leg.

"Think of that," said his wife, "Order of the Siam Crown, 4th Class."

For a moment a snapshot of Milton Ashley, somewhere in the tropics, in a stained pith helmet, flickered on the Colonel's mind like a scene in an old movie. Then he closed his eyes and said, "If they're shedding I guess I better stay back here—" and stepped from the kitchen into the room at the back. It smelled —perhaps it would always smell—of the food the cats had eaten, the Red Heart, the canned milk, and above all the cantaloup. The delicate aroma of the ripe melon seemed to be part of their coats.

35

They were both a little unbalanced about cantaloup.

While the cats were shedding they lived in the room at the back of the apartment, off the bathroom, and while this was going on the Colonel lived there himself. There was a bed, on which they all slept, an imitation tree where the cats used their claws, and the French doors where they could all take the sun. The cats had been trained to use the bathroom like the guests. The black cat, Jackson, used the tub, standing erect with one paw on the soap dish, rocking back and forth like a man in his cups. The white cat, Georgia, used the newspapers spread on the floor. They were placed there, one sheet at a time, as the Colonel went through the morning paper while seated on the stool. Whenever guests were anticipated, they were taken up. The Colonel's wife had opinions on this subject, but she had never expressed herself directly except by the use of assorted air deodorants. A bottle of Air-wick sat on top of the water closet. Guests who had not been warned about the cats sometimes had the surprise of their lives when the black cat, Jackson, raised his head and peered from the tub. Superstitious people, like the Colonel himself, sometimes went to considerable trouble to give Jackson the undisputed right of way.

At the back of the room were the wide French doors, and in the summer the Colonel would leave them open, sometimes swinging his chair around to face the view. He seldom went out on the balcony itself. It had a low, scarcely knee high, railing, the drop to the garden was sixty feet, and the Colonel had never been much of a man for heights. Elevator stops, and the view from high windows troubled him. The Colonel's wife, however, on particularly humid summer evenings, would take a straight back chair and seat herself on this balcony. She seemed to have no feelings at all, but it sometimes troubled the Colonel, seated there in the room, just to look at her.

On the walls of the room—it had been some time since the Colonel had looked at them—were pictures of cats his wife had once given him. Things she found in magazines, or clipped from the rotogravure. Kittens tangled in lengths of wool or string, many views of Chessie asleep in her berth, and both kittens and cats who had fallen in love with dogs, slept with them, ate with them, and on occasion used the dogs as a transportation system for crossing streets. There seemed to be no end of such pictures

36

and the Colonel's mail, while he followed the army, brought him a fairly large selection once a month. There was seldom a letter, as his wife could use the borders of the pictures for suitable comments, and send him a good deal more, as she said, for less. Nearly all of the Colonel's personal mail came 4th Class. His mother sent him clippings of Milton Ashley, his wife sent him cats.

Perhaps his long spell in bed, facing one window, had strengthened the Colonel's inclination to sit and watch whatever happened to be going on. It had something to do with the pleasure he found in cats. The cat, Jackson, for example, liked to be stroked after meals, as an aid to digestion, but the cat, Georgia, did not like to be touched. Why was that? Georgia would sit at his feet, facing away, as intact and withdrawn as a Sphinx, while the Colonel, stroking the belly of Jackson, would gaze at her. It had been a test, from the start, of his self control. If he put out his hand she would leave, retire to the bed. A stranger might think that this cat, Georgia, had little or no use for men, or what his wife described as human company. But he would be wrong. Let the Colonel get up and walk to the door, and the white cat, Georgia, would walk there with him; let him shave in the bathroom and Georgia was there, seated on the stool, listening to his electric razor hum, curling her lips delicately when he held it near her face. Antisocial? No, she simply didn't want to be touched. Quite a bit like Mrs. Foss, put it like that. She didn't really care to be touched either, to have her back scratched, or her belly rubbed. The Colonel had an understanding with the cat, Georgia, and it might be that the challenge, for that was what it was, brought out the best in both of them.

Seated there in his room the Colonel could hear the sounds of applause from the jackpot program that came, as he knew, from the floor below. It helped remind the Colonel that he was home. The lights still flickered when the refrigerator motor switched on. He smoked, blowing the smoke directly up his face, like a curtain, as the cat, Jackson, didn't care for it. Eyes wide, he stared at it ominously. Nothing aroused him more than the click of the refrigerator door. The Colonel's feelings about Georgia ranged from the highest admiration to the kicks that he gave her, as if by accident, under the bed.

37

3

The Colonel was still in bed, propped up on a pillow, watching Jackson lick the cereal cream from his fingers, when he heard his wife answer the telephone. "I'll see if he is in," she said, a remark that she usually reserved for the army, then came to the door to his room and spoke to him.

"A Mr. Tabori—" she said.

The Colonel tried to think.

"He said to tell you he was calling for a Mrs. Kopfman—"

"Oh—" the Colonel said, and threw back the covers. That was unusual—he realized that without lifting his eyes to his wife, who stood there, soberly, watching him.

"You're here, then?" she said.

"Oh yes, I'm here," the Colonel said, but she waited a moment, watching him fish for his slippers under the bed. "Tell him I'll be right there," the Colonel said, and continued to fumble with his slippers until she walked back through the apartment. He sat there until he heard her say, "Colonel Foss will be right here," and then he was.

"Hello—" he said, clearing his throat, "Colonel Foss speaking."

"This is Tabori" said the voice, "Tabori at The Regent Arms," and the Colonel raised his eyes, then lowered them to the floor. "Mrs. Tabori didn't realize," he went on, "who you really was, she didn't really get it. If she'd known who you was she

39

would have asked you about him."

"I see," the Colonel said. "Well, that's too bad."

"She's hard of hearin' you know."

"I know—" said the Colonel. "If Mrs. Tabori would like to ask a few questions—"

"I suppose you know how women are."

The Colonel turned to glance at his wife, as if to reassure himself about women. "What would Mrs. Tabori consider a good time?"

"She's busy all morning, but she gets an hour off between two and three. Two and three," he repeated, "she gets an hour off."

"I'll try to make it around half past—" the Colonel said, then realized, suddenly, that he was making an appointment to see a chamber maid. "I can't be too certain, Mr. Tabori."

"That would be fine," the bellhop said, "and it will certainly please Mrs. Tabori," then, as if cut off on the line, he hung up. The Colonel waited, as he felt there was some mistake. He put the receiver back on the hook, then stood there, his hand on the phone, as if he expected the bellhop to call him right back. Jenny Lind, scratching around in her cage, sprinkled him with seeds.

The Colonel's business was his own affair, and his wife never troubled to ask him about it, nor did she now, when he turned and looked at her. She was holding the phone pad she had picked up.

"That's Hyman Kopfman's mother," the Colonel said, "she remarried a Mr. Tabori." He thought it better not to mention that Mr. Tabori was a bellhop. He waited for his wife to speak, her eyes appeared to focus on a spot low on his neck. There were times that the Colonel felt his wife accepted things too easily, considering how really complicated they were. "Mrs. Tabori," he said, "that is, Mrs. Kopfman, is now over at The Regent Arms."

"The Jewish people are taking it over," said his wife. She said this flatly, a matter of fact that held, for her, no particular interest. There was nothing implied, nothing concealed, and the Colonel had the curious feeling that it gave the observation greater weight. That it seemed to come from some impersonal source.

"Mrs. Tabori is employed there," the Colonel said, as if that might make it better, though he didn't add in what capacity. Something about his wife's silence led him to say, "Mrs. Tabori

40

is a very fine woman," though he had no idea, really, what kind of woman she was, other than deaf.

"What does she want with you now?" said his wife, and walked around so that the bird cage hung between them. It was swinging, slightly, and she put out her hands to steady it.

"When I dropped off that package," the Colonel said, "—I told you I was going by with a package—Mrs. Tabori didn't realize who I was. She's pretty hard of hearing. She didn't seem to realize that I knew her son."

"Cheep, cheep, cheep," said his wife to Jenny Lind, "cheep, cheep, cheep."

"When she learned who I was," the Colonel said, "she naturally asked him if I wouldn't drop back and speak to her."

"She's moulting," his wife said, and from the bottom of the cage, while Jenny Lind fluttered, she removed several seedy feathers with black tips. The Colonel walked to his room at the back. He stood there with the door ajar for a moment, a towel folded over his arm, as his wife had a way, after thinking things over, of summing them up. But she said nothing. She seemed to be concerned with Jenny Lind. The bird hopped around the cage, the perch was rocking, and the Colonel was troubled with an old notion that if *he* was a bird, he would find his wife's face frightening. Up close, peering through the fragile cage like that. It was possible the bird—the Colonel walked into the bathroom as if to finish the thought in private—thought that *she* was free and the Colonel and his wife were behind the bars. It was another example of the kind of thing that illness and idleness had done to the Colonel, turning his mind to such childish fantasies. In the bathroom he faced the mirror without looking at his face.

At one time the Colonel would stroll as far as the Brooklyn Bridge, walk out on it, and stand where the breeze would stir the flaps of his uniform. The view, of course, was spectacular. The Colonel suffered his usual discomfort of heights, but he was drawn out on the bridge as his tongue was drawn to the hollow of a sensitive tooth. The discomfort he felt was melancholy and pleasurable. Out there he sometimes felt the curious remoteness he had often felt as a boy when he sat in the kitchen with the stereopticon cards in his lap. The nearness and farness of life deeply troubled him. On one of these cards, a street scene in Paris, the river and the trees were like objects in amber, removed from time. This river would always flow, and no wind would blow these leaves from the trees. But near the center of this card was the figure of a woman with blurred feet. She was not of marble. She was alive, going somewhere. Had she been to see her lover? Was he at this moment waiting for her? Would he go on waiting, as this woman went on walking, until this occurred? The frailness and mystery of this woman who had no name, no face, no destination, seemed to embody, for the Colonel, the frailness, mystery, and anxiety of life. All around her was Paris, like a city of marble, and the trees cast heavy, permanent shadows, but the feet of this woman, and the flowers of her hat, were blurred. For a passing moment, like the shadow of a bird's wing, she moved from one curbing toward another, but leaving no trace among these permanent-seeming things. Perhaps this was why the Colonel remembered her. As he would a cat crawling among ruins and monuments. It was why, perhaps, he preferred those views where time, like movement, seemed to have stopped, and he had to look twice to remark the change in anything. The figures might be blurred, but the Colonel liked to keep them on the cards.

At the back of the Colonel's mind, and nowhere else so far as he could determine, there lived a one-eyed, one-armed Captain of the US Army, retired. The Colonel sometimes had a lunch, a drink, or a quiet game of billiards with the Captain, who had learned, in spite of certain handicaps, to play quite well. He was known as "the Captain" and resided at "the Club."

"The Captain and I—" the Colonel would say, facing the wall in some phone booth, "are going to have a quiet little game at the Club."

The Colonel's wife had never questioned it. It was understood, if not implied, that the Colonel had managed to have with the Captain the kind of comradeship that she liked to associate with men at arms.

"Give the Captain my regards," his wife would say, and although she was not a sentimental person, there was sometimes just a touch of it in her voice. The thought of old soldiers playing together appealed to her.

Another man might reserve this kind of thing for the most

important moments in his life, but either the Colonel had none to speak of, or held a very different notion as to what they were. Perhaps his wife, in her own fashion, understood that. She had no objection to his having a little innocent fun.

The last time the Colonel had called upon the Captain he had bought himself a half pound bag of mixed nuts, several cigars, and attended a newsreel theatre. He took a seat in the loge, where, after eating, he could smoke. The Colonel had a special weakness for war newsreels as they took him to faraway places, and he was able to participate, actively, in foreign battle scenes. If he sat through such a newsreel two or three times—as he was inclined to, if it was a good one—he could give you a lively description of the conflict, the deployment of the forces, and he could point out for you the important landmarks of the site. The cathedral that was bombed, or preferably gutted, the hill that was stormed and subsequently leveled, and the effect of the ruins as seen from a plane, or a nearby rise. Other men would have exploited such a talent, but the Colonel usually found it enough to correct small errors, or add an interesting detail to the stories he heard. These passing remarks, modestly put forward, had a curious effect on certain discussions, and were apt to overshadow the reports of men who had actually been there. Heroes, some of them, with well earned medals on their chests. It was a curious fact that these brave men had a very poor conception of the battle, the strategic situation, or just what had taken place. It seldom compared with the Colonel's newsreel view. Not many of these boys had been trained in tactics, and the Colonel's picture of Monte Cassino, which he had slowly mastered in a week of newsreels, gave some of them their first idea of what they had been through. It had also helped the Colonel to get through a war he had fought in the mud around Shrevesport, Louisiana, until the chemical blast had made him a casualty. The newsreels had been important to his morale, and whenever his morale seemed to be important he would step in a phone booth, somewhere, and call up his wife. "The Captain and I—" he would begin, and nine times out of ten she would interrupt him, in a good natured way, to ask him to be sure and give the Captain her best. He was usually home by half past nine or ten o'clock.

As Mrs. Tabori was resting, the bellhop led the Colonel down the corridor to her room. The Colonel had the feeling, perhaps due to the light, that she had not moved since he had last seen her, and that she had turned her back on the world, like one of his cats. When the door clicked shut she raised her eyes, but it would be wrong to say that she saw the Colonel. "AHHHH-hhhhhh—" she said, and appeared to be pleased with what she saw. There were many sentiments the Colonel did not trust, but only one that made him embarrassed: loving kindness. The luminous eyes of Mrs. Tabori glowed with it. The Colonel recognized it—when he had to—as a front for something else.

"The work here is taxing," the bellhop said, "she's all worn out."

The word *taxing* impressed the Colonel as a strange one, but good. He, too, would like to find things *taxing*, rather than merely hard.

"She's up at five every morning," continued the bellhop, "and for a woman of her age—" What would that be, the Colonel wondered. Was she prematurely aged or wonderfully preserved? "She is looking for somethin' less taxing," the bellhop added.

"She does housework?" the Colonel inquired.

"If it's not too taxin', Colonel." He let the Colonel reflect on that. "Nobody seems to want an older type person any more. All they seem to want is younger persons, without much experience."

"I know, I know—" the Colonel's head nodded. As a matter of fact he *did* know. His wife did not like frail, aging people around the house. Did she hire people, she said, to do the work herself?

"It just so happens," the Colonel said, "that I might know of something in the way of house cleaning, but of course that's just more work, not less."

"It might not be so taxing, eh?"

"Strictly speaking," said the Colonel, "it's not a house but an apartment."

"How many are you?" said the bellhop, "how many of you in this apartment?"

"Just myself and wife," said the Colonel, "we have four rooms, not at all crowded," although he meant to avoid mentioning these details. If the truth were known, the Colonel didn't care

44

for domestics around the house, as he had certain old fashioned notions about a man's private life.

"No children?"

"No, no children." The Colonel was aware that things had gone too far, but was uncertain how to put a stop to it.

"If there are no children," said the bellhop, summing up, "and if there is just you and your wife, the cleaning might not be too taxing."

"It isn't a full time position," said the Colonel, "so you can see there is not much of it. Mrs. Foss also likes a person who can cook."

"I'd have to talk it over with her," the bellhop said.

"It goes without saying," the Colonel said, "that Mrs. Foss does her own hiring. I just happen to know that there might, soon, be an opening."

"For an old friend," the bellhop said, "she'd be glad to do what she could." He gave the Colonel such a twisted, cloying smile he had no idea what he meant. An old *friend*? What did the nervy little bastard mean? The Colonel had only time to follow him back to the lobby, where—like an old friend—the bellhop gripped his hand, shouting in a voice that even the clerk could hear that "Mrs. Tabori would do anything she could, *anything* she could, for old family friends."

45

4

The Colonel stood in the bathroom: the tapwater ran cool and chlorinated over the blade, reserved for toenails, with which he had managed to cut himself. When the phone rang he turned off the water, opened the door of the bathroom, and stood there with the cut finger in his mouth.

"Who is this speaking?" his wife said, then, "Just a moment, I'll call him." She did not call him, however, but merely stood there looking at him.

Taking the finger from his mouth, the Colonel said, "For me?"

"Does he have to call at this hour of the morning?" She closed her gown at the throat, indicating what hour of the morning it was.

The Colonel walked to the front of the apartment, picked up the phone. "Colonel Foss speaking."

"Colonel, this is Tabori," said the bellhop.

"Oh, yes, Mr. Tabori—"

"I've talked it over with Mrs. Tabori," said the bellhop, "and she says she'd be glad to do you the favor." Into his mouth, which stood open, the Colonel put his bloody finger. Then he removed it and said, "We're not asking a *favor*, Mr. Tabori, what we have in mind is a part time position."

"I just mean she wouldn't think of doing housework for just anybody, I mean she'd only do it for a friend of the family."

"As I think I said," replied the Colonel, "this is naturally up to Mrs. Foss."

"You think I don't know how women are? You think I don't know that?"

"All I mean is—" the Colonel said, but it was too early in the morning for such a discussion.

"I know how they are," said the bellhop, "don't think I don't know *that*."

"Hold the line a moment," said the Colonel, and then turned to look for his wife. "It's about Mrs. Tabori," he said. They had talked about her the night before.

"I'm not sure that I want an old woman," she replied.

"Mrs. Tabori—" said the Colonel, "is not an *old* woman."

"You get these old people in your home and you're just likely not to get them out. You can't evict them. You can't evict them if they're old and sick."

"If you don't care to see her—" the Colonel said.

"I didn't say I didn't care to see her," she said, "I said if she was old it might be hard to get her out of the house."

"What time could Mrs. Tabori stop by?" said the Colonel, speaking again to Mr. Tabori.

"So long as she has this job," said the bellhop, "she's only free from two to three. That's why it's so taxing. That's why she needs different work." His voice was so high it carried across the room to the Colonel's wife.

"If she can't do anything taxing I might as well do the work myself," she said.

"If she'd like to come by at two," said the Colonel, "I'm sure Mrs. Foss would be glad to see her. You have the address?"

"I got it from the book, I looked it up in the book just to make sure it would be handy."

"We're just down the street, but it's quite a little walk up."

"Nothing like the walking you do around here," the bellhop said.

"I suppose not—" said the Colonel.

"I walk around twenty miles a day," said the bellhop. "I kept track once. It ran a good twenty miles."

"Well—" said the Colonel, then looked around the room as if for a way out of the discussion. "Well—" he repeated, then he heard the click as the bellhop hung up the receiver. The Colonel stood there, listening to the buzz.

"I don't care for aging people—" said his wife, then paused before saying, "are you bleeding?"

The Colonel held his finger to the light and saw that he was. Some vague scruple, now that she was watching, kept it out of his mouth. He held it upright, like a pointer, walking slowly through the house to the bathroom, where he turned on the tap-water. He soaked the finger for several minutes, applied antiseptic powder and a band-aid, then came to the door and said, "She'll be here at two o'clock."

There was no answer. His wife was nowhere in sight. The Colonel walked through the front room, peered into the hall, then came back to stand at the door to the kitchen.

"Oh, Claudine—" he said.

"I heard you the first time," she said.

The voice came from beneath the dining room table that the Colonel faced. He had learned not to question acts that came so naturally to his wife. Between the table legs, he could see that she was down on all fours, dusting something.

"Claudine—" he said.

"Never you mind, Mr. Army," she said. "You think I'd ask an old woman to do something I wouldn't do myself?"

Between lunch and half past three the Colonel sat in The Regent's lobby reading the papers, in particular the Want Ads dealing with able bodied domestic help. Somewhere along the line he had made a mistake. The mistake had something to do with this fellow Tabori, a bellhop, and the manner in which he had taken, so to speak, the initiative. He called before breakfast to grant them favors, to question them. It had given the Colonel's wife the feeling that he and the bellhop had been conniving, which was understandable, as the Colonel felt that way himself. He felt a certain relief, as a matter of fact, to get out of it. It would be hard on Mrs. Tabori who certainly needed work less taxing, but there was something about Mr. Tabori that made the Colonel ill at ease, though it was only a feeling and nothing he could put his finger on. It might have been different, for example, if Mr. Tabori had not been a bellhop, as the Colonel was sensitive to the meaning of uniforms. For certain personal and highly

49

complicated reasons the Colonel not merely felt ill at ease, but at a curious disadvantage when dealing with a bellhop's uniform. It did not describe, as it should, a circumscribed area. The bellhop was free, like the domestic help or the photographers from certain magazines, to reveal certain facts it was the business of *some* uniforms to conceal. The Colonel's uniform, particularly. So he felt relieved, as his wife was a person who could deal with Mrs. Tabori as a woman, and with Mr. Tabori as a bellhop, if he called up again.

On the third floor landing, where he stopped to rest, the Colonel thought he heard the voice of his wife, a little loud and on the gay side, as it was apt to be over the telephone. So as not to disturb her, he used his key to open the door. But the room was empty, except for the twittering of Jenny Lind. At the back he heard his wife's voice again—pitched high, as if calling to him— and he stepped forward to say "it's just me, dear," which was what he usually said. He stopped between the folding doors, however, as he could see through the apartment to the kitchen, where a strange woman sat at the table, sipping tea. A tea bag string, and twirling label, dangled from the edge of the cup. The Colonel recognized the cup, imported from England, and therefore seldom used, but not the woman who held it. She wore a long shawl, of fragile material, and a wide brimmed hat that concealed her face, a piece of tattered veil hanging loosely at the side. Around the top of the hat there were red and green berries, thin strips of veil, and soiled paper flowers that inclined in his direction, as if from a draft. The woman's dress was black, but of so fine a material that her slip showed through, as if illuminated, and led the Colonel to raise his hand, reflectively, to his eyes. On her feet— or rather on the foot thrust toward him, as her legs were crossed —was a high button shoe of fine kid leather, but the heel was gone. Or rather not gone, but going, the tip worn to a round knobby point like the tip of a cane. The Colonel had seen such clothes, if not such a woman, step from the doors of certain brownstone houses, like ghosts, or living remnants of an elegant but vanished past. There was something about these women that appealed to him. They had lived, or the clothes had lived, in an orderly, civilized world, such as the Colonel would have preferred to live in himself. A world of parasols, to put it briefly, where the sun glistened on the water, on waving flags, on the faces of children, but the eyes of women were withdrawn and serene beneath the parasols. The Colonel stood there, uncertain as to whether to take a step forward, or backward, when the woman's hat, like a miniature landscape on a revolving stage, moved around to face him, the flowers vibrating, and the eyes beneath the brim, more luminous than ever, fastened on him.

"Is that Mr. Army—?" he heard his wife say, and when the woman gave no answer, just sat there soberly gazing, his wife came to the door. Her face was flushed in the manner that made her more attractive than ever, and she was wearing the apron she had bought for Libby Bird. Holding up an English muffin, she said, "Would you like to join us, Mr. Army?"

For a moment the Colonel stood there, saying nothing. Then he noticed that the hat, with the berries and flowers, was nodding up and down in a pumping manner.

"You might as well join us," he heard his wife say, "as Mrs. Tabori and I have reached an agreement—haven't we?"

"Ja-ja," the woman replied, her voice hoarse in a manner that indicated she didn't often use it.

"Come, join us," repeated his wife, "you've got to live with both of us now, you know."

Somehow it had slipped the Colonel's mind that this Mrs. Tabori was first a Kopfman, that the Kopfmans were from Vienna, and that in Vienna life might be on a higher plane. He had been told that. He could now see that it was so. In the shadow of her hat, with its wide brim, the luminous eyes had about them an unearthly quality. Earthly, but extremely refined, was the shawl about her narrow shoulders, the fine lace at her wrists that looked brittle as paper, the alligator bag with the green copper buckles and clasps. Mrs. Tabori's elegance was now shabby, but no doubt it had been very fine at one time, and in one place. Perhaps it was this that appealed to the Colonel's wife. She had a taste for this type of refinement—the looted demi-tasse spoons were of the same period—and she knew good materials even when she found them in a strange place.

Strangest of all, however, the really peculiar thing about Mrs. Tabori was not her dress, her high-button heelless shoes, nor her luminous unearthly gaze, but that she sat there with her thin legs crossed, sipping tea. It troubled the Colonel. It revealed the unsuspected chambermaid. As her flowing skirt was long, one foot was covered, but the other thrust forward to where the Colonel could see an inch of the calf, if one could use the term for such a leg. The toe of the boot tapped at the air with the beat of her heart.

Without her uniform—the green skirt and blouse of The Regent Arms chambermaids—Mrs. Tabori looked even more fragile than usual. That was the shabby elegance, perhaps, with the hat that made her head seem too large for her body, like the drawings of elves the Colonel had seen in nursery books. The same was true of her hands, which were too large for the wrists, and the feet that seemed too large for her legs. The Colonel found it unclear, from where he was sitting, whether to see Mrs. Tabori as a single person, or merely the focus for a collection of loose parts.

The Colonel had his tea, two buttered muffins, and heard from his wife that Mrs. Tabori had been kind enough to give them two days a week of her precious time. Mondays and Fridays, to start. Mrs. Tabori said *ja-ja* to this, like a muffled bark. When his wife asked him if he had any suggestions, the Colonel said no, no he couldn't think of any, but he did hope that Mrs. Tabori was fond of cats. She said she was, or rather she nodded, the ja-ja being too much of an effort, and the berries on her hat made a dry sound among the crisp paper leaves. The Colonel brought Jackson in, explaining at the same time how the white cat, Georgia, who was something special, neither cared to be stroked nor picked up. Whether Mrs. Tabori followed that was not clear; she had the habit, common to those hard of hearing, of nodding her head and smiling agreeably to whatever was said. She stroked the head of Jackson, who did not seem to mind, and with her claw-like fingers scratched him on the spot that made his tail, in spite of himself, grow stiff and rise. As Mrs. Foss led her off Mrs. Tabori had to stop to gaze at Jenny Lind, who began singing, and it was clear that she had a special feeling for birds. The Colonel waved from the kitchen, then turned away as in the strong slanting light she seemed to be transparent, a wiry metal frame on which a shawl had been draped, a thin dress had been hung. Nor did he lean from the window, like his wife, to see in what direction she was going, or how, in a pair of heelless shoes, she managed to walk.

"Mondays and Fridays," said his wife. "We've got to be careful not to overtax her. You can have your lunch out."

52

5

Several times during the night he thought he heard a mouse in the room. He would sit up, listening, and hear the bird scratching in the cage. The cage hung directly above the day-bed, and the bird would swing on the creaking perch, or scratch seed from the bottom of the cage that fell on his face. He moved his head from that end of the bed to the other. He had been under the impression that the bird sat quiet all night, under the quilted hood, and he lay there wondering if the bird, too, had marked the change in the house, in the sleeping arrangements, and in the inhabitants. Birds were said to be clever, and quite a change had taken place.

On the ceiling of the room the Colonel could detect the changing signal lights on a far corner, and several times he sat up in bed to look at his watch. Or he stood at the window as if waiting for the dawn. At one point he had a drink of water, letting the tap water run into his hands, and drinking from the palm as he used to drink at the pump, as a boy. It was not easy, however, and some of the water got into his nose. When he sneezed his wife spoke to him, so that he knew she was not sleeping either, and he wondered if Mrs. Tabori, in her new bed, was also awake. He thought he could detect, at regular intervals, her whistling snore. In the long night he neither slept, nor daydreamed, nor turned his mind to the pressing problems that had occupied him, so intensely, the day before. He merely put in the time, he turned his head to noises, he fought off or gave into a bad throat tickle, and when dawn came he didn't trouble to get up and look at it. He lay there remarking how the room filled with light. Flies trapped between the screen and the window began to buzz. Gradually, the traffic began to flow, and as if the quiet had kept him awake, as the noise increased the Colonel began to doze. He slept, for an hour perhaps, and he dreamt that he carried a small black bag which contained the leg, the arm, and the tongue of a person who was following him. He awoke when the bird began to sing. In the chair beside his bed, in her bathrobe, his wife sat peeling an orange, prying at the skin with her long finger nails. In her lap was a napkin, for the peel, and as she tore off a piece of the skin the Colonel could see the fragrance, like a puff of smoke, blend with the air.

"Yes, Claudine—" he said. When she came to him it indicated there was something on her mind.

"I've been thinking," she said, and put a piece of the orange into her mouth. She meant only what she said. She said she had been thinking. "I've been thinking of what we could do with your room," she said.

He thought she meant decorating, as she had never been pleased with the furniture or the wallpaper.

"It's up to you, Claudine—" he said.

"If I took yours, she could have mine, and you could have this one to yourself."

He went back over the statement, just to make sure that he had heard it right.

"Do I understand, Claudine—" he began.

"I don't want to lose her right now, I don't want to lose her right when I'm getting results."

The scent of the orange, at that time in the morning, troubled him. It crossed the Colonel's mind that the smell of fruit, of one kind or another, was the smell of the apartment. He didn't like it. It always made him think of flies.

"Claudine—"

"You don't really use your room, there's no one in it but the cats."

"I spend every night in that room," he said, hardly knowing why he troubled to say so, and not realizing what he had said until too late. But it didn't matter. She took such statements literally.

"The Simmons day-bed is a better bed," she said.

54

"If what you have in mind, Claudine—"

"I can't afford to lose her right now when I'm getting somewhere," she replied. With Libby Bird, with all of them, there was a point where she seemed to be getting somewhere. As it never lasted, he was not sure what it was.

"I'll have to speak to Mr. Tabori about it," he said.

"Mrs. Tabori is now in our employ," she replied. The word employ, as she used it, was not the ordinary word. It meant that Mrs. Tabori, bag and baggage, was now in their hands. Although that was what the Colonel had had in mind, now that *she* had it in mind he was not so certain.

"I think we'll have to be tactful," the Colonel said, "a man like Mr. Tabori might—"

"You're a man," his wife replied, "you speak to him," as she sometimes said, "cats don't wear feathers," which summed up her feelings on the complicated subject of cats and birds. She put the last slice of orange in her mouth, folded the peel in the napkin, and arose. At the bathroom door she turned to say, "I'm running a bath for Mrs. Tabori, you want in here first?"

"What time is it?" the Colonel replied, but before she could answer, the telephone, right there beside the Colonel's head, began to ring. He let it ring, like a man who was deaf, until he saw his wife, still at the door to the bathroom, making motions indicating that he should answer it. So he picked it up and said—"Colonel Foss speaking."

"Colonel, this Tabori," said the nasal voice. The Colonel saw, on his mind's eye, the well tailored rear of the mincing dandy with the walk like a jockey. "Hello, you there Colonel?" the bellhop said.

"Yes," said the Colonel, but it cost him quite an effort. He placed one hand at his side, to support himself on the bed.

"Was on the late shift last night," went on the bellhop, "an' when I got in I found that Mrs. Tabori—"

"Mrs. Tabori spent the night here," the Colonel said.

"Ohhhhhhh—Well, I'm relieved to hear that."

"There was a good deal to do, and Mrs. Foss thought it might be late for a—"

"I wasn't worried, Colonel, wasn't worried at all, as I knew she was in good hands, but when I came in late and found the bed empty—"

55

The Colonel drew his head away at the word *empty*, coughed into his hand. "—just so long," the bellhop was saying, "as she don't find it too taxing."

"Mrs. Tabori is not up yet," the Colonel said, lowering his voice to make the point clear, "but if you would like to speak to her—"

"Let her snooze, let her sleep, what she needs the most is a good long sleep. Probably sleeps better with you than she does with me." Once more the Colonel drew his head away. Did he hear the bellhop snickering?

"It just so happens," the Colonel said, "that we do have an extra room."

"I'm glad you brought it up," the bellhop replied, "as it sure makes her work less taxing. She don't have to get up early. She don't have to leave. I didn't bring it up myself because so few people have extra room."

"We really don't *have* it," said the Colonel, "but we can make it. On the rare occasion we can make it."

"I understand that. Don't think I don't understand that, Colonel. I'm just saying it sure makes it less taxing for her."

"Should I have her call you?"

"No, don't bother. Don't make yourself the trouble. It's just that when you come in and find the bed empty—"

"Sure, sure—" said the Colonel, interrupting. "Well, I think Mrs. Tabori is pleased."

"I think her sleeping with you is fine," the bellhop said.

"Well, we'll have to see—" the Colonel replied, lidding his eyes to shut off the picture. "We'll have to see, Mr. Tabori," but the bellhop was gone. Did he make a practice of quietly hanging up? The Colonel sat there, the phone in his hand, until he noticed that his wife had come back into the room to look at him. When he raised his eyes she drew her robe closed at the front. Nothing personal, however, merely a reminder that his wife was a woman, and that the Colonel, slouched on the bed, was a man.

"What does he want now?" she asked.

"Just wondering about his wife. When a man's wife is gone, overnight, he might wonder where she is." He stopped there. She took no offense, however, so he said, "He seems to think it's all right."

"What is?"

56

"Her sleeping here," the Colonel replied. He watched his wife take the brush she was holding and with an absent, practiced air, like one of the cats, slowly stroke the hair on one side of her head.

"What am I to say to him?" the Colonel said, as he felt the same vague irritation with her absorption, her remoteness, as he sometimes felt with the cats. At such times he might push, pinch, or throw a pillow at one of them.

"You're a man, you speak to him," she said, and took a step forward, into the light, to examine the hairs she had caught in her brush, but she gave no indication as to what she saw. Were they grey? More than usual? It was hard to say. She tipped her head and began to brush the other side.

"Well, if that's what *you* want—" said the Colonel, and the emphasis he placed on the you, very firmly, made him stop and think. The day before, it was what *he* wanted. What had changed? He couldn't put his finger on it. "Well, if you're sure it's what you want," he repeated, and raised his eyes, though he heard nothing, to gaze through the door to the kitchen just as Mrs. Tabori, in her nightgown, crossed the back room. She was wearing a night cap, with a tassel, and perhaps it was the black cat, Jackson, tagging along, that made her look like a Halloween witch.

6

On a sheet of good quality embossed paper, the Colonel wrote to Mr. Tabori in regard to Mrs. Tabori, his wife. He made a proposal that would take her off his hands. He worded this in the disinterested professional manner of the official army correspondence, and agreed to pay, along with her board and room, twenty dollars a week. This would be a dead loss, more than likely, and go into the bellhop's evil pocket, but five dollars a week would be put aside for her, personally. Saturday night and Sunday she would be free, as the Colonel put it, to do as she liked, even if this meant spending the night at The Regent Arms. There was some indication, however, that she would do nothing of the sort. It was difficult to tell just how much Mrs. Tabori understood, and how much she didn't, but she had shown no inclination, on her free weekend, to leave the house. Simple minded people, the Colonel felt, were apt to be that way. They liked to find a rut they considered satisfactory, and stay in it. On another level, Mrs. Tabori didn't seem to distinguish between one day and another, as she never read the papers, nor did she get up and go to church. On alternate days she would leave empty milk bottles at the hall door, or pick full bottles up, but that can be learned without knowing what day it is. The Colonel, that is, had caught on to that himself.

He mailed this letter on a Monday, and having received no answer by Friday, he assumed that the bellhop considered the arrangement satisfactory. The Colonel began to feel that way himself. There had always been a problem about breakfast—of more than ten years standing, that is—as the Colonel and his wife approached the meal differently. The Colonel had habits he had acquired in the army, which seemed to suit him personally, and his wife had habits she had acquired while living alone. She was inclined to dawdle over her breakfast. The Colonel would shave, dress, then take his seat in the corner of the booth, painted peacock blue, and sometimes sit for an hour, maybe two hours, watching his wife play with the food. She would say, "Would Mr. Army like a nice hot cereal?" and though he knew better he would say yes, as it might be cold outside and she wanted it herself. She didn't believe in the three minute cereals, of course, and sometimes he would sit there for forty-five minutes before she got the oatmeal, or whatever it was, to the right consistency. Then when she did serve him, he would eat too fast, and be through with his cereal, and ready for his coffee, by the time she had put the sliced fruit on *her* cereal, and taken a seat. Even the eggs didn't work out much better, as he liked his own soft, and while they were hot, and she liked them on the well done side, and ate them when they were cold. If he smoked at the table, she didn't like it, and though it cost him a good deal of effort he had always known better than to get up from the table ahead of her. As a result, he drank too much coffee—as she pointed out.

Breakfast had always been a problem until he spent the night on the day-bed, and to simplify things Mrs. Tabori brought it to him on a tray. It kept him out of the kitchen, which was small, out of the bathroom during the rush hour, and out of what his wife referred to, every morning, as *us girls' way*. It had been strange to hear his wife talk like that. Part of it might be due to the fact that Mrs. Tabori was so small, almost childlike, and perhaps simple minded in an innocent childish way. As she was more or less deaf, however, it was harder to explain why his wife, without raising her voice, spent the day talking to her. The Colonel had never thought of his wife as the talkative type. Most of this talk was so low that the Colonel was unable to follow it, and Mrs. Tabori as a rule said nothing at all. She was apt to say *ja-ja* in a dead silence, or pronounce the AHHH, very loud and clear, when one of the cats rubbed against her legs.

The day began at a quarter past seven when his wife would

put on the water for the coffee, and Mrs. Tabori would run Mrs. Foss' bath. While Mrs. Foss was in the tub, Mrs. Tabori would prepare the Colonel's breakfast of two soft boiled eggs, buttered toast, coffee, and orange juice. The Colonel would receive this food on a tray, which he would shelter with his napkin as Jenny Lind, in the cage above his head, was very active in the morning. After eating, still in bed, he would have a smoke, and if the coast was clear to the bathroom he would retire there, with the cat Jackson, and shave and dress. While he was in the bathroom, Mrs. Tabori would make up the bed. The Colonel was then free to sit with his cats or leave the house for the morning paper and a walk. If he left the house, he would call from somewhere saying that he had a luncheon appointment, as he found it too exhausting to climb the stairs more than once a day. Around five o'clock, as a rule, he would be back. During the period his wife was breaking in new help, the evening meal was apt to be very good, since she prepared it herself. The Colonel found it worth the trouble to be on hand.

After the meal the Colonel's wife would help Mrs. Tabori alter her clothes. What a collection she had! Even the Colonel recognized the remarkable elegance of her wardrobe, although it was distinctly out of fashion. The materials were of a quality no longer available on the open market. Obviously enough, a woman with such a "trousseau" had not been destined to be a domestic. Somewhere along the line, and a very good one, she had shared a cultured background. Why not? That was hardly uncommon for those who pulled up stakes and came to the new world. One moment they had servants waiting on them, and the next they were the servants. *C'est la vie*—a phrase the Colonel had picked up in The Regent's bar.

To sit and watch these two ladies sewing appealed to some buried refinement in the Colonel's nature. Something attractively feminine in his wife came out in the skillful way she used the needle, pinning it, when not in use, in the soft material of her blouse, with the thread dangling. This was done without thinking, but with such precision her bosom was never punctured. This simple, graceful gesture filled him with admiration. What a talent she had! For Mrs. Tabori he felt the purest amazement that her knobby fingers could repair the finest laces. With the threaded needle between her pursed lips she reminded the Colonel

61

of a nest-building bird. How right that parallel seemed. A pair of clucking birds, repairing their nests. They made a strange pair, the two ladies, and the Colonel observed them with satisfaction, some annoyance, and a puzzling sense of disquiet. The Colonel looked on as if from a window across the street.

So much for the Colonel's evenings. His afternoons were spent in numerous bars. "The same, Colonel?" Yes, it was always the same. On a stool at the bar, munching the peanuts, he was solitary in a babble of voices. He enjoyed the blurred rumble of the music and the glow when some woman inhaled a cigarette. The flame would create, as if out of the darkness, a lidded eye or a moist painted mouth, and this fragment was superior, the Colonel knew, to the face as a whole. Just as the dangling phrase, or the occasional grunt, was superior to the whole conversation and led him to feel that something important was being said.

Not that it mattered, of course, since the Colonel was merely killing time, and between wars he had a lot of it to kill. The same time, and it appeared to die the same death. He took the same walk, he read the same papers, he regarded his face in the same mirrors, but something new had been added—the Colonel was no longer bored. On arising in the morning, even before arising, he was aware of a disquieting feeling, not quite apprehension, more like a troubled expectancy. Not an unusual feeling, you might say, for a man who had been hit from behind by a pie truck, but he felt it all the time, and in a more disturbing way, this dangerous intersection he carried around in his mind. The day itself seemed to be spent crossing this imaginary street. On getting out of bed he stepped from the curbing, and the sense that anything might happen remained with him, like a portent, until he was once more back in bed. Even there he merely put it aside, as he did his pants and his shirt, knowing that in the morning he would arise and put it on again. The same things, therefore, were all a little different, and on those days when nothing happened the Colonel would have liked an even longer day to loaf. Another five or ten minutes, another hour, might bring to pass what he had waited for.

A Thursday evening, between nine and ten o'clock, the Colonel had stepped out to get Friday morning's paper. He had taken a slow stroll around the block, and on his way back he saw the ambulance parked out in front. The red light on the top blinked on and off. Several people, with their dogs, had gathered, and a policeman, club in hand, stood with his back to the apartment house. The Colonel got there just as the door swung open and two ambulance attendants, in white jackets, carried the body of a man from the hallway into the street. They carried him feet first, and the Colonel recognized the large knobby shoes of Kluger, the janitor, as egg shaped holes had been cut in the toes to allow for his corns. Bits of garbage clung to the soles and Kluger's right hand, that hung as if forgotten, still clutched a piece of wilted lettuce. The Colonel also remarked the bottle in his hip pocket, and that when a man dies in his cups the alcoholic flush is slow to leave his face. The dark wet stains on the front of his shirt were another indication that Kluger, as was his custom, had been drunk. A lacy suds had dried about his lips. The food stains on his knees seemed to indicate that he had first spilled the garbage, then followed it, head over heels, down the stairs. He often did. Everyone had predicted he would kill himself. Collecting the bags of garbage so incensed Kluger, a sick and embittered man, that on the garbage days he would get himself good and drunk. It nerved him up to abuse certain tenants, and make passes at the women he might find, at that time in the evening, on the stairs. There had been many complaints, but it was clear there would be no more of them.

The Colonel stood with the crowd, he watched the ambulance leave, then he stepped forward and asked the policeman what terrible thing had just come to pass. He learned that the janitor, Kluger, had just broken his neck. He had been drunk, and had fallen, with the garbage, from the top of the stairs. The Colonel remarked what a sad thing it was, but how, as a tenant of the building, he couldn't say he hadn't expected it. So everybody had said, the policeman replied, and stepped to one side so that the Colonel, key in hand, could enter the garbage littered hall. Melon rinds, eggshells, carrot tops and bits of lettuce were strewn on the stairs. The Colonel went along the railing, which was relatively clear, but on the third step from the top he stooped for something that glistened in the hall light. A piece of torn silk cord, to which the silver clasp was still attached. The Colonel stood there, turning it about in his hand, until he heard someone on the stairs behind him and stepped to one side to let Mrs. Tabori, with a waste basket, slip by. Waste paper was not garbage, it had to be emptied by the tenants themselves into the large canvas bags that hung on the basement wall. Mrs. Tabori had emptied hers, and she held it before her, her eyes on the stairs, as the Colonel pressed himself to the railing to let her pass. Whenever she was busy Mrs. Tabori had a preoccupied air. It might have been a perfect stranger, rather than the Colonel, that she passed on the stairs. Her customary glance, luminous as ever, was also somewhat impersonal, and as she went by, her head tipped to see where she was going, he noticed the red line, clean as a knife cut, at the back of her neck. When she made the turn, at the top of the stairs, he saw that this line did not appear at the front, and he looked at the broken piece of cord he held in his hand. With the other he took a firm grasp on the railing before he looked back at the man at the foot of the stairs. The policeman remained in the door, his back was still turned. His club hung idle, like a limp tail, between his stout legs. The Colonel made the turn of the stairs, walking slowly, and somewhere between the third and fourth floor he slipped the hand that held the cord into the pocket of his coat. On the fourth floor the door stood open, and his wife, who had heard the commotion, let Mrs. Tabori by and then stood there, waiting for him.

"What in the world—" she began, then waited for the Colonel to wipe his face with a piece of Kleenex. The night was warm, and the climb had left the Colonel's brow damp.

"Kluger—" he said, and took off his hat to press the Kleenex to his forehead. "Fell with the garbage, looks like he killed himself."

"Well, we all knew he would," his wife replied, and though the Colonel was not surprised, his wife's directness found him unprepared. He admired this quality of her mind. He admired it very much.

"It was just matter of time," she said, when she saw that he was not ready with an answer, then she turned back to the window at the front, and leaned out. The crowd was gone, but two or three people, with as many dogs, still hung around the entrance, and the Colonel wondered if the sniffing dogs smelled something. Anything strange, that is, anything weird or unusual. What a man could sense and sniff out, certainly a dog could smell. Here was something that had been in the air for weeks, one moment like an odor, another like a tremor, but only now

64

was it something that the Colonel could see and touch. A piece of torn silk cord, a clean red line at the back of a neck.

Did she strike him? Or did he merely lose his balance and fall? Toppling over slowly, at first, like a statue, then a windmill scene of flailing arms and garbage, without a cry, perhaps, without a sound but the dull thudding on the stairs. She had been on her way down so she continued, making her way through the strewn garbage, then stepping over (how else?) the body sprawled at the foot of the stairs. A little Eva, a weirdly comical figure mincing her way through the scattered rubbish, and though the picture made him smile the Colonel opened his eyes when the hair began to rise along the back of his neck.

"It was just what I predicted," said his wife, and let the window down with a bang.

7

That had been Thursday evening, and Saturday morning the Colonel lay awake, his eyes on the ceiling, waiting for the telephone to ring. It rang at twenty minutes past seven, as usual. The Colonel's wife was still in her bath, and Mrs. Tabori had just opened the refrigerator door: the Colonel cleared his throat, coughed, and said, "Colonel Foss speaking."

"This Tabori," said the bellhop, "hope I didn't get you up."

"Why, hello Tabori," the Colonel answered, then realized his slip. "What's on your mind, Mr. Tabori?"

"Wonder if sometime today I could have a word with you." He was smoking in the phone booth: the Colonel could hear him blow out the smoke.

"Let's see, this is Saturday—" said the Colonel. "Saturday is a pretty crowded day."

"Can't tell you over the phone," the bellhop said, and the Colonel placed his hands over the receiver, as if he could keep the voice of the bellhop bottled up. *So he knows it,* the Colonel thought, *he knows all about it*: his mouth was so dry he was unable to speak.

"Hello," said the bellhop, "you there, Colonel?" He was there. "You want to come here, or you want me to come over there?"

"Look—" the Colonel wet his lips, but said nothing, absolutely nothing.

"Any place you like," said the bellhop, "but I can't tell you over this phone. You know what I mean, Colonel?"

The Colonel wagged his head. Realizing the bellhop couldn't see that, he said, "Say you meet me in the St. George Bar?"

"St. George, eh? What time, Colonel?"

"Say around four o'clock."

"I'm only off at two fifteen," said the bellhop.

"All right," replied the Colonel, "make it two fifteen."

"See you at the St. George," piped the bellhop, and although the Colonel drew his head away, he heard the sharp click as the receiver went down on the hook.

The voice of the bellhop—more than what he said, or what he might know—troubled the Colonel the way the wail of a siren troubled him in the street. There was just a touch of panic, and a stronger will than the Colonel's own seemed to advise him to stand still, ignore the danger, and perhaps it would pass. The Colonel had observed this same voice speak to his cats. If they were trapped, if they were tangled in a cord, if they were caught half in and half out of something, there would be a moment when they would simply ignore it, and the tension would relax. The cat, Jackson, would endeavor to wash his face, the cat Georgia might even purr for a moment, as if this show of calm, of indifference, would wish their troubles away. It's all in your mind, this voice seemed to say, just relax, take it easy, and the monster will vanish, and it was amazing how many times this proved to be true. The trap would open, the cord would untangle, the head would slip out of the noose the moment the tension, the paralyzing fear, was relaxed. There were, however, those times when the pause didn't work. The magic spell was invoked, the silence was observed, and one might even think that the monster had vanished—often a mistake. The Colonel had observed this in the fuse-like twitching of a cat's tail. For when the powers of light had failed, then the cat called upon the powers of darkness, he gathered his forces, and he made one final, exhaustive try. A voice that reduced all other voices to whimpers had spoken to him.

All this had nothing to do with the Colonel except for the fact that it had crossed his mind, and when something crossed his mind he had nothing else to do but dwell on it. He had observed the cats, and in the last few weeks he had remarked a certain resemblance, when the phone rang, between the cats and himself. He was inclined, in certain situations, to play dead. He was in one of them now. He would shave, dress and eat, as if nothing had happened—but he was privately terrified. When the time came he would appear at the St. George Bar. If a trap, he would walk into it. There was a potato bin under the sink where the cats were frequently trapped. But had they learned to stay clear of it? They had not. If the door to the bin was left open, there might be a yowl, or there might be nothing—nothing but a missing cat. There was a voice behind the potato bin that beckoned to them. It was not unlike the voice that spoke to the Colonel, as he had nothing to gain, everything to lose, and one of these times the trap would close on his head or his tail. The powers of darkness spoke to him more persuasively than the powers of light.

If what the Colonel wanted was peace of mind he might have left the torn silk cord at home, or dropped it from the Brooklyn Bridge. He thought of that. As a matter of fact, it led him to walk out on the bridge. Out over the water he was seized with the fear that he might jump from the bridge himself. This strange obsession left him with the feeling that only the torn piece of cord really mattered, and that *he* mattered, if at all, only in relation to it. The cord was there in his pocket when he took a booth in the St. George Bar, one near the door so he would spot the bellhop when he came in.

Otherwise, he might not have recognized him. The bellhop did not appear in the monkey suit he wore in the lobby, although the faded red pants showed at the bottom of the raincoat he had slipped on. He wore leather gloves, and a tight fitting cap that emphasized the smallness of his skull, and gave him the look, the Colonel thought, of a hack driver. He walked like a bellhop, however, and in the gloom of the bar, after the light in the street, he sailed past the Colonel without seeing him. It was necessary for the Colonel to let it be known that he had business, of one sort or another, with the character who was wearing, under his raincoat, a pair of red pants. At the bar, in the mirror as it happened, Mr. Tabori picked up the signal and like an alerted bellhop, with a bag in each hand, he hurried across the room. He took the seat facing the Colonel, and as he did so, with a practiced gesture, he adjusted the tight fitting cap to the shape of his head. The Colonel had observed that ball players did it while playing for time.

"Well, what will it be, Mr. Tabori," he said, and tapped his glass with his fingers.

"I always take the same," the bellhop answered, winking, "only less and less water in it."

The Colonel managed to appreciate that, and put a smile on his face. He was also aware that the bellhop, who was wonderfully at ease in a lobby, showed signs of being jittery in a high class bar. Perhaps he was no longer accustomed to sitting down. He removed the cap, peered at the band, then shaped it carefully to his head, but this time more in the manner of a self conscious boy.

"You sure this is private enough, Colonel?" He gave a tug on his cap that almost concealed his face. Was it the gloom, the thin cloud of smoke, that made his face look sinister? "I'm thinkin' of you," the bellhop said, "I'm thinkin' of you, Colonel, not myself."

With his free hand—the other remained in his pocket, fondling a pillbox—the Colonel raised his glass, and had a long drink. He had taken gin and tonic. He wanted his mind to be clear. Now he put the glass down and said, "What's on your mind, Mr. Tabori?"

"It's really on *your* mind, Colonel," said the bellhop, then paused as the Colonel was coughing. The Colonel stopped, wiped his lips and forehead with a paper napkin, cocked his head to one side and said, "You mean Kluger?"

"Who's Kluger?" The bellhop leaned forward to stare at the Colonel, the smile on his face.

"Just a man in the apartment building," said the Colonel. It calmed him to feel he had the upper hand.

"A man, eh?"

"Why, yes—"

"If I was you—" said the bellhop, clutching the sides of the table, "if I was you, I'd keep the rest of 'em out of it."

"Out of what?" The Colonel smoothed the flap on his right hand pocket. Now that he had asked it, the Colonel wanted to take it back. He didn't want to know. He would rather go on in the dark. But he had said it, so he repeated, "Out of *what*, Mr. Tabori?" Then he leaned back as in that way he was able to brace himself.

70

"I'm willing to handle it for fifty a week," the bellhop said.

For a moment the Colonel felt he was going to be sick. The feeling passed, and he said, "You can do what for fifty, Mr. Tabori?"

"I can keep it quiet, I can handle it for fifty."

The Colonel pressed the palms of his hands to the cool sides of the glass. He had no idea what the bellhop had in mind, but he had felt vaguely guilty, of some unnamed crime, all of his life. Was he now on the verge of relief? As if after years of struggle, of hiding out, he had finally brought himself to the bar of justice.

"I'm not just proposin'," the bellhop said, "to take your fifty and give you nothin'. I'm just proposin' that Mrs. Tabori is worth fifty a week."

Blackmail, thought the Colonel, and the shock of the word gave him a sharp thrill of pleasure. "Before we go on—" he said, with a calm that was no longer affected, "I'm going to ask you to tell me just what it's all about."

"You're kiddin' me, Colonel."

"No, I'm not kidding you," the Colonel said.

The bellhop fanned the cigarette smoke from the air, stared at the Colonel's face. The Colonel's sense of pleasure-pain was so great that he did what he could to prolong it. He closed his eyes. He waited for the earth to quake.

"You want it straight?" the bellhop said, and the Colonel signified that was how he liked it. He leaned back from the table and held himself straight. "I understand—" said the bellhop, "that you don't sleep with your wife."

The Colonel opened his eyes. He was about to ask what that had to do with the situation, when he saw the answer, clearly, on the bellhop's leering face. The same face Kluger had once turned to him from the top of the stairs. The Colonel raised his glass, took a swallow, pressed the napkin once more to his forehead, then said, "I take it you are suggesting—"

"For fifty bucks a week," the bellhop interrupted, "I'm suggesting nothin'."

"You think you have a case?" the Colonel replied.

"Mrs. Tabori needs the money. She needs the dough. She's got to start layin' it aside."

"I'm perfectly willing," the Colonel said, "to lay aside a weekly sum for Mrs. Tabori. But as for blackmail—"

71

"I'm askin' you not to push me," the bellhop said.

"If you expect the world to believe, Mr. Tabori, that a woman the age of Mrs. Tabori—"

"I'm goin' to ask you not to push me, Colonel. I'm goin' to have to ask you that."

"It seems to me," said the Colonel, "you don't have too much of a case."

"Colonel—" said the bellhop, took off his hat, puffed out the crown, then returned it to his head. "—you still pushin' me, Colonel?"

The Colonel sat with a quiet smile on his face. He took a crisp dollar bill from his pocket and put it in the saucer at the center of the table. He looked at his watch, he took a final swallow of his drink.

"O-kay, Colonel," said the bellhop, "don't say I didn't warn you."

The Colonel shrugged his shoulders, indicating that he couldn't care less.

"If you have anything to say, Mr. Tabori—"

"All I got to say," said the bellhop, interrupting, "is fifty bucks a week is not much money. It's no money at all considerin' what you got in the house."

"If you think you've got a case—" said the Colonel, but he didn't go on, no, he just sat there, as it was the bellhop who was pushing to his feet. He didn't leave, however, but leaned far forward, propped on the table, as if he meant to see the sweat on the Colonel's face.

"You're a smart man, Colonel," he said, his voice down to a hoarse whisper. "You'd think Mrs. Foss—"

"Mr. Tabori—" said the Colonel, rising, "we'll leave Mrs. Foss out of this." From his full height the Colonel looked down, and like a bug beneath a rock, the bellhop looked up.

"You think we ought to, Colonel?" the bellhop said, and gave the Colonel a sidelong leer, "don't you think she ought to know she's got a *man* in the house—in case she wants one?"

That was all. On that Mr. Tabori closed his case. With his characteristic gesture he tugged at his cap, gave a curl to the brim, then gave a twist to his head, screwing it around, as if it had worked itself loose on his shoulders. "I told you not to push me, Colonel," he repeated, as the Colonel had placed one hand on the table, and the bellhop seemed to mark some change in his face. "I *warned* you, Colonel—" He wagged a finger at him, then he turned and went off, half running, as if he had heard the bell in The Regent Arms lobby ringing for him. After standing for a moment, the Colonel resumed his seat.

In the gloom of the bar, as at the back of a cave opening out on the lunar landscape of the alcoholic, the Colonel reflected on the course of his life and the strange consoling enormity of the crime. He was relieved to find that it seemed crime enough. That he felt both debased and gratified.

The Colonel had once been at camp on the plains, within a mile or so of a railroad junction, and on the hot summer nights he often lay awake listening to the trains. The mile-long freights would stop for water, then start up again. This manoeuvre—the first jolt of the engine, and the passage of that impulse along the train—left its mark, not apparent at the time, on the Colonel's character. Through it he saw the logic in certain meaningless events. Hearing the first thrust of power down the tracks, he would rise on his elbow, like a man appointed, and wait for that impulse to reach the caboose. He could see the caboose, with the tail lights flickering, totally unaware of the chain of events, like doom itself, marching toward it along the tracks. He could predict, within a fraction of a second, when it would strike.

This experience gave the Colonel a sense of exhilaration, as if he gazed at this world from another planet, and could make out future events, like cloud shadows, moving across the landscape to their destination. The Colonel's temperament being what it was, it led him to conclude that all unforeseen events, if seen in perspective, were in one way or another predetermined, and to this curious circumstance men gave the name of Manifest Destiny. He observed that most men got along without it, like freight cars parked on a siding, while the course of events, the main forces of history, passed them by. He had even felt himself of this number—in a fairly long life there had been no jolts, or shocks, to speak of—until the pie truck had hit him from behind. In a matter of months his manifest destiny had caught up with him. He delivered himself, with the black fiber bag, into its hands. The moment the Colonel had set eyes on the bellhop, he had

73

heard, as he had on the plains, the whistle of his future blowing thin and wild far down the tracks. The impulse had been given by the pie truck, and now the jolt had finally reached the caboose. This was it. This was the crossing bell he had been waiting for.

Nor did it cross the Colonel's mind that the bellhop might be pulling his leg. Or that a man into woman might prove to be somewhat complicated. The crime hardly mattered, after all, what really mattered was the connection between the locomotive, the whistle down the tracks, and the caboose. Every man felt, the Colonel was sure, the lurking furtive guilt that he had been feeling, and the need to attach this sense of punishment to some crime. Whether Mrs. Tabori was man, woman or monster was irrelevant. As the ice slowly melted in the drinks that were brought him, the Colonel thought he could hear, like a whistle on the plains, the long far cry of his manifest destiny. The jolt that he felt had been in his own caboose.

A little after six the Colonel left the bar, bought himself two Coronas in the lobby, then stepped into a booth to call his wife. He was in a pleasurably terrified state of mind. He knew it would pass, but he wanted to hold on to it. He would tell his wife that he and the Captain . . .

"Claudine," he said, "the Captain and I—"

"Where have you been?" she interrupted.

"I—" the Colonel replied, but he hardly knew. Never before had she troubled to ask him that.

"He's called several times," she said, "and he wants you to call him back."

"*He?*" said the Colonel, calmly, as if he didn't know.

"I said you would call him," his wife replied, and the Colonel stood there, saying nothing. "Where are you?" she asked, "can't you call him from there?"

"I'm over here at the Club," the Colonel lied.

"You can call him from there," she said, and although the Colonel had nothing to say, nothing at all, he was struck by the fact that she hung up. He left the booth, circled the lobby, then came back to the telephone girl and asked her to get him a Mr. Tabori, at The Regent Arms. It took her quite some time. During the discussion she once swung around to look at him. When she put him on the line he said, "This is Colonel Foss speaking."

74

"This Tabori," said the bellhop, "you doin' anything right now?"

The Colonel didn't know.

"I can't get off," the bellhop continued, "but I can step outside if you wanta walk by. I'll be at the door. All you do is walk by."

"What's on your mind?" the Colonel said.

"This is on *your* mind," the bellhop replied. The Colonel coughed. "I told you not to push me, Colonel."

The Colonel was standing in the booth: now he sat down.

"If you can make it in ten minutes," said the bellhop, "I'm due for a smoke in about ten minutes," and that was all of that. The next voice the Colonel heard was the operator's. On his way out of the building he stopped in the drugstore and had a cup of black coffee, then he lit a cigar, left a dime on the counter, and walked out on the street.

The lights were on beneath the sidewalk awning when the Colonel, cigar in hand, stopped beneath the awning to take a look at his watch. Before he raised his eyes, or felt the need to, the revolving doors spun around and the Colonel caught the flick of red as the man came down the steps. He let him hurry off, then followed him down the street. There was light in the sky, but in the shadow of the buildings the Colonel might not have recognized the bellhop as he had slipped on the raincoat again, and the tight fitting cap. The Colonel drew up beside him when he stopped to light a cigarette.

"I got to get back—" the bellhop said, blowing out the smoke as if it burned him, and flipping the match, the head still glowing, into the street. The Colonel waited, but the bellhop seemed to find it hard to begin.

"What's on your mind—" the Colonel said.

"All I want to say is, is that if I was you I wouldn't talk about it. I wouldn't let on. I wouldn't let on at all, you know what I mean?"

The Colonel wasn't sure. "Mr. Tabori—"

"It's just between you an' me, Colonel, it ain't for Mrs. Foss, it ain't for Mrs. Tabori. What I told you you got to take for granted, you know what I mean?"

75

"You mean—?"

"I mean if I was you I wouldn't fool around with Mrs. Tabori. I mean I wouldn't spy on her, go snoopin' around her, you know what I mean?"

"It seems to me—"

"I know how you feel," the bellhop said, "you probably feel curious, I suppose I'd feel curious, but you got to take my word. I advise you to take my word for it." To emphasize the point, the bellhop's hands went up to his cap, shaped it to his head.

"She doesn't like the idea?" the Colonel said.

"If she *gets* the idea—" the bellhop said, "that anybody thinks she isn't *Mrs.* Tabori, if she gets the idea, then you can leave me out." He put his right hand at his side, the palm down, and wagged it from side to side. "Out—" he repeated, "then you can leave me *out.*"

"You're the one that gave me the idea," said the Colonel. "I didn't have it. I can't say that I believe it."

"I know—" said the bellhop, "I know—but don't let *her* get it."

"She doesn't like it?"

"She don't believe it." The bellhop threw up his hands, like a man at the end of his rope. "You got to take my word, Colonel," he said, "you got to take my word."

"You mean to tell me—" the Colonel said, "that Mrs. Tabori—that *he*, thinks he's Mrs. Tabori?"

"That's what I mean," said the bellhop, "and that's what she wants to think."

"I don't think I follow it."

"I'm not askin' you to follow it," interrupted the bellhop, "an' I don't give a damn if you believe it. What I'm doin' is tellin' you what you *better* think." His voice had got high, and his head thrust forward, screwed to one side, as if it hurt him. The fingers of one hand tapped firmly on the Colonel's chest. "It don't make it any different for you," he went on, "whether she thinks it or whether she don't. I suppose you can see that—?"

"I can see that," the Colonel replied. He could see that, but what troubled the Colonel was not so much what he felt himself, but what the bellhop seemed to feel. He seemed to feel scared. The Colonel could feel it himself. "I can see that—" the Colonel repeated.

76

"All of that don't matter a crap," said the bellhop. "What matters is what I'm tryin' to tell you. What matters is what she thinks herself!" He put the palm of his hand flat on the Colonel's chest. It was clear he thought he had made an important point.

"She can be pretty sharp, I suppose—" said the Colonel.

"HA!" said the bellhop, and the sound came from him as if he had been squeezed. "HA!" he repeated, then made a quick pass through the air with the flat of his hand, using it like a blade, and made a sharp sound with his mouth. As he made this sound, his neck seemed to snap. It gave the Colonel such a start that he put his hand toward the bellhop, who seemed to be living in fear of something. He even felt, strange as it seemed, in league with him.

"Between you and me, Colonel—" the bellhop said, resting his hand on the Colonel's sleeve, "just between you an' me it's worth more than fifty a week."

That was vague, God knows, but the Colonel got the gist of it. Whatever the bellhop's fear the Colonel recognized it as superior to his own, just as his own was superior to his fear of the day before. They were both, the Colonel realized, exalted by the same dread, and at sea in the same boat. To show that this was not lost on him the Colonel said, "There's Kluger. Where does Kluger fit into this?"

The bellhop closed his mouth, his eyes, and put his hands over his ears. As he naturally resembled a monkey, the impersonation was very good. "I don't wanta know, don't wanta hear," he said.

"There was nothing, really—" the Colonel began.

"Don't tell me, Colonel. I don't wanta know." He opened one eye, but he kept his ears covered.

"It's nothing—" said the Colonel, and waved his hand to show that he was willing to forget it.

"I got enough on my mind," the bellhop said, "I don't wanta know." He looked down at his wrist watch, then added, "Well, I gotta get back, Colonel—"

"I'll start the fifty tomorrow," the Colonel said.

The bellhop wagged his head from side to side, slowly, indicating that the fifty was indeed a small matter. "Colonel—" he said, "If *she* ever got wind that for a measly fifty bucks—" but there he left off, as if a voice had spoken to him. He glanced over his shoulder, fit the cap to his head like the case to a bowling ball, jerked down on the brim, then went off toward The Regent Arms. The Colonel stood there, lost in thought, and before he struck the match he was holding he had a look, in both directions, along the street. In the apartment where Mrs. Tabori now lived the lights were on.

The Colonel waited till those lights were off before he went upstairs. He left them off, and quietly undressed in the dark. The May night was warm, a gramophone in the room across the street played rumba music, and he lay out on the day-bed listening to it. From the room at the back, where the door stood open to catch whatever breeze might be stirring, came the long damp whiffle that his wife produced when she lay on her back. The picture in no way aroused the Colonel—nor the knowledge that her night-gown, like a lifebelt, might be in a wad around her shapely waist. She would be there, her knees drawn up, and in the room beyond her was this Mrs. Tabori. Did she sleep on her back? The thought led the Colonel to lid his eyes. It also crossed his mind that an act of boldness, in the manner of an absent minded husband, would settle the problem that now lay so heavily on his mind. It would hardly be illegal for a man to enter his wife's bedroom. It could easily be explained as the act of a distracted sleep-walker. That might settle his own mind, of course, but it might unsettle the mind of his wife, who knew how poorly such an act really suited him. Who would explain to her that he had been within his rights? No, it would merely make it worse than ever, and as the bellhop himself had observed, it was worth a good deal more than fifty a week. He had got a lot of blackmail, it seemed to the Colonel, very cheap.

Whether this creature was man, woman or monster, the Colonel and the bellhop now lived with it. What the bellhop had done was sell him a share of his predicament. This blackmail was not for money at all, but for company. That was what the bell-hop had sold him for the fifty a week. It had been too much for the man to live alone with his fear. So now the Colonel had it— he had at least part of it—and perhaps this night the bellhop would sleep as he had not slept in years, while the Colonel lay awake. It made the Colonel smile (he raised both hands to his face as if to hide what he was thinking) as he had been alone himself, and now for fifty a week he, too, had company.

8

That weekend was the first that Mrs. Tabori asked to have off.

The Colonel was served his breakfast, as usual, and half an hour later, as he stood in the bathroom, he heard his wife say good-bye, good-bye at the front door. She then came back through the apartment to the kitchen, where she rapped on the bathroom wall. She would go out of her way to find a wall to rap on, rather than a door. The Colonel unplugged his razor, and she called, "Vivian and I are going to do a little shopping, so if you and the Captain—" Her voice trailed off as she had walked from the kitchen. Vivian Oakley was an old friend of Mrs. Foss' that the Colonel, somehow, had never set eyes on. They got together on the maid's day off, and sometimes made excursions together if a war was on.

The Colonel waited a moment for further instructions— he could hear his wife closing the back windows—then he plugged the cord in again, finished his shave. He was in the tub when she tapped on the wall but said nothing: he sat there, waiting, until the front door closed with a bang that rattled the shower curtain rings. He got out of the tub, wiped his feet, then hurried toward the front, a towel around his middle, just in time to see his wife leave the building and cross the street. She carried an umbrella, a sign that she would be gone all day. The Colonel watched her out of sight, then he came back through the apartment, through the kitchen, into the room where his wife now slept. The cat, Jackson, came forward and spoke to him. The cat, Georgia, was not in sight, until the Colonel saw, through the door at the side, the bed reflected in Mrs. Tabori's bureau mirror. On the bed was Georgia. Her back was turned to the door. The Colonel walked to this door, he would have entered, if his own undressed reflection, like a fat picked chicken, had not distracted him. The towel that he wore bore the monogram of a high class Los Angeles hotel. Also in the mirror, and on the top of the bureau, were dozens of miniature animals, a menagerie of glass, pottery, and carvings from soap and wood. Birds of the air, beasts of the field, and creatures of the sea were all gathered together, arranged in pairs, and each pair had its place in the line that wound around the bureau top. They stood as if waiting the signal to march.

All of this the Colonel saw in the mirror, but where they were headed was not reflected, where they were going did not show up in the glass. To see where that might be the Colonel had to enter the room. One foot in the door and the Colonel could see the toy wooden ark that was propped at one end of the bureau top. Into this ark, up a ramp, they were marching two by two. Not the right two, however, not what you would call a pair by normal standards, as a big cat and a bird stood side by side, there on the deck. A snake and a field mouse were on their way up the ramp. Paired up with the wooly lamb was the tiger, side by side were the wily fox and the rooster, arm in arm marched the city kitten and country mouse. Was anybody missing? The Colonel wasn't sure. He leaned forward, his weak eyes squinting, and searched the assembly for Adam. There was none. How about Eve?

On the ark itself, glued to the paper deck, was a childish figure with a painted face, the plastic arms upraised to welcome the creatures that marched up the ramp. Her button eyes were wide, she smiled with a red painted mouth. Missing was Noah, and others of his kind. Here were only the bird kind, the beast kind, the glass, pottery and wood kind that would march in strange pairings into the ark.

Over the long weekend Mrs. Tabori was gone, but Monday morning, at quarter past seven, the Colonel got out of bed to

80

answer the door buzzer. When he spoke into the tube he heard the faint trapped sound of a dying AHHHhhhhhhhhh.

The Colonel buzzed the door several times, but when there was no voice in the tube he opened his door and peered into the hall. "Oh, Mrs. Tabori—" he called, in a moderate voice, but there was no answer. The echo, drawn out like a wail, came back to him. He put on his slippers and his robe and started down the stairs.

On the second floor, as he made the turn where Kluger had toppled to the bottom, the Colonel went along the railing, his right hand gripping the bannister. In the dim hall, gloomy as a bar room, the frosted glass in the door was like a skylight, and the Colonel could make out a shadowy figure in the vestibule. It appeared to be deformed, like a hunchback, and rose from the floor no higher than a dwarf. Nothing moved, there was no sound, and though the Colonel reached the foot of the stairs, he was unable to remove his hand from the knob on the bannister. His legs trembled, and his feet were rooted to the floor. The Colonel recognized the symptoms, he had heard them described as the product of an overwrought imagination; the hand at his side was another man's hand that happened to be resting on the polished knob of the bannister. There he remained, in a trance of fear, until a delivery boy entered the vestibule, sounded one of the buzzers, then pushed open the door. The hump-backed monster visible through the glass proved to be Mrs. Tabori, seated on a large denim duffle bag. "AHhhhhh—" she said, and rising from the bag smoothed the wrinkles from her clothes.

The duffle bag appeared to be packed with very dirty clothes. As the Colonel picked it up, and gave a tug on the cord, the soiled sleeve of a shirt dangled from the side, and a pair of dirty brown socks seemed to ooze from the top. The Colonel pressed them down with a firm hand.

"Now you go on ahead, go on ahead—" he said, and waved his hand at the wrist, as he did for children, to indicate that Mrs. Tabori should go on without him. While her eyes were on him he appeared to study the duffle bag. It was very high, bulky, and it was something of a mystery how Mrs. Tabori, who was small and frail, had got it this far. "I'll take care of this," the Colonel went on, "you go on ahead, as I think Mrs. Foss—" and there he stopped, as he could hear Mrs. Foss speaking for herself. With

Mrs. Tabori he raised his eyes, peering up the stairwell two, three flights to where the head of Mrs. Foss, like one painted on the ceiling, gazed at them.

"Ahhhhh—" said Mrs. Tabori. From the foot of the stairs, as she made the wide turn on the landing, the Colonel saw that the top of one stocking hung down like the flapping boot top of a cavalier. He closed his eyes, and when he opened them again she was gone.

The duffle turned out to be heavier than he had thought. On the second landing, where he stopped to rest, he decided to hoist the bag to his shoulders, and as he doubled over he heard the drawcord pop. As from a swelling horn of plenty the contents of the bag showered around his feet. A soap box and a hairbrush rattled down the stairs to within one step of the bottom, and the handle of the hairbrush made a noise like a saucer rocking to a stop. The Colonel was so anxious to recover the pieces he hardly noticed what they were. One thing he picked up was a cheaply framed photograph. The glass in the frame had cracked, but it had not fallen out. It looked like it might, however, so the Colonel slipped the frame into his bathrobe pocket, and returned the rest of the stuff to the duffle. One of these articles was red, with brass buttons in pairs down the front. The Colonel stuffed it in, then took it out, held it up to the light as if to see better, then dropped down on the stairs as if his legs had given out.

Seated there he had time to examine the photo behind the cracked glass. Four frail boys, of assorted ages, but all somewhat dwarfed in stature at the feet of a woman dressed in the elegant manner of Mrs. Tabori, the young Hyman Kopfman cushioned in the folds of her skirt. The Colonel simply lacked the nerve to look into the eyes of anybody else.

The Colonel took it upon himself to replace the broken glass in Mrs. Tabori's frame. He often passed a photo shop on Flatbush Avenue with the engaging sign

WANT ANYTHING FRAMED?

which he considered prophetic of his own situation. The clerk in the shop, a young man of foreign extraction, seemed to admire

82

the photograph very much. In contrast to the vogue for the candid camera, he liked the old studio portraits. The older the better. He was quite out of his mind about daguerreotypes. He believed that priceless "family documents" like this one should receive the most considerate attention. Details that appeared to be lost should be restored. He pointed out to the Colonel how two of the faces, somewhat sepia in tone, might be strengthened, and that the cheeks of the child in her lap would surely profit from a touch of color, applied by hand. The Colonel felt obliged to explain that he preferred the infant's sallow appearance. It was more like him. He admitted to knowing the child quite well.

"It's nearly thirty years old," the clerk said. "If you don't catch it now, it'll soon be too late." How did he know that? There was a date on the back of the photograph. Also on the back, in pencil, one of the children had written this legend—

> Paul Kopfman
> Soldier of Christ
> Larrabee YMCA
> Chicago, Ill.
> USA
> The World
> The Universe

"You're Mr. Kopfman?" the clerk inquired. He merely wanted to identify the order.

"Make it Colonel Kopfman," the Colonel said, in one of those little twists that prove so hard to explain. Did he feel the need to conceal something, or was it merely an urge to play at being somebody else? Leaving the shop he felt that Hyman Kopfman would be quite amused by such a turn of events, his old friend the Colonel actually bearing his name. How easy it was, really—if circumstances so contrived—to leave the house as one person and return as another. Were there many who did it? He fancied that there probably were. Some who were bored: some who feared— as was said—for their lives. Wondering into which category he fit, the Colonel paused on a corner to glance at the papers. A single word—not the headline—caught his eye.

BELLHOP LEAPS OR
FALLS TO DEATH

He had time to read the sketchy details before the light changed. This particular bellhop, identified by name, and described as an employee of The Regent Arms, had either fallen or leaped into an open elevator shaft. That was not unheard of. It was known to happen when the doors were propped open. His body had lain at the bottom of the shaft for two or three days. Police were looking for his wife, who seemed to be missing, and one or two friends not as yet identified.

Would one of them be Colonel Foss? It was not implausible. Colonel Foss had been seeing quite a bit of Mr. Tabori, and had given him a check for the sum of $50. "I'm goin' to ask you not to push me," the bellhop had said, but clearly somebody had.

Strange to relate, this incident calmed, rather than aggravated the Colonel's mind. It defined his position, it cast him in a new role, and it revealed a certain order in all the disorder, as he had known for years that he was, above all, a nonidentified man. An accomplice, as yet unnamed, to crimes yet to be discovered. He had not been there to see or hear Kluger fall, nor had he seen the bellhop vanish into the elevator shaft, but he was the connection, he was the link of order, between these strange events. He had heard the whistle, he had felt the jolt in the caboose. An innocent man, he walked about the streets with a piece of torn silk cord in his pocket, and on his mind, as on a blackboard, the bellhop's last prophetic remarks.

"If she ever got wind—" he had said, "that for a measly fifty bucks a week—"

And she had got wind. That was the gist of it. It was this wind the Colonel felt blowing on the back of his neck. Was that why notorious thugs and much admired wanted men—like Humphrey Bogart and other adventurers—walked about with the collars of their raincoats up behind their ears? It was hardly the Colonel's style, and would surely not appeal to his wife—but was it, any longer, her affair? Not so long as Mrs. Tabori had no reason to feel herself pushed.

Was it wonder that made the Colonel a philosophical man? From the bridge, where he could see in all directions, he tried to look upon himself with a certain detachment, as well as upon the inhabitants of the apartment he could see on the Heights. The French doors were open, and one of the women was airing out clothes. Whose clothes were they? The Colonel tried to face it

84

philosophically. The woman was his wife and when she leaned on the railing the Colonel would lower his eyes, or close them, as he felt uneasy about the narrow railing on the balcony. The sight of anyone leaning on it troubled him.

The Colonel passed the day out on the bridge, thinking, and when he got hungry he walked over to Manhattan, where he had a hot dog at one of the stands facing City Hall Park. His mind, without much trouble to himself, had made itself up. Or rather Mrs. Tabori had made it up for him. Whether she was man or woman was of no importance until somebody questioned her, and the only man left to do that was the Colonel himself. The only way to avoid that was to go somewhere. Anywhere. To put temptation, both his own and Mrs. Tabori's, out of sight.

In the shops around the square the Colonel bought a raincoat, a dark pair of polaroid glasses, and a tin of aspirin which he put in the pocket of the coat. In the Pennsylvania station he had a haircut and a manicure. Standing in line at the ticket window he heard a woman down the line return a reservation, and when he reached the window he inquired what reservation this was. An upper berth to Chicago? The Colonel settled for it. Wherever he was going, he would need his sleep. Ten minutes later he boarded the train and gave to the porter a short telegram to his wife.

CALLED AWAY LINE OF DUTY.
URGENT EMERGENCY. LOVE.
ROGER.

In the pocket of his coat, when he searched for his ticket, he found the receipt for the photograph. The clerk had written the name of Kopfman on the front of it. It was not a common name, it stuck in the mind, and even in a city as big as Chicago there might not be too many of them in the directory. It was interesting, the Colonel thought, that he held in one hand the name of Kopfman, in the other a ticket to Chicago, where the Kopfmans were said to be from. It made him smile. At one time he would have thought it merely a coincidence.

9

The last time the Colonel had been in Chicago he had spent several hours in the planetarium, where his wife had taken him during the wait between trains. It had been a hot, mid-summer day, and on arriving in the station she had purchased a guide book that described the planetarium as dark and cool.

That had been years ago, before the war, but it served to remind him that for the first time in his life he was now a free man. Neither his mother, his wife, nor the army now had charge of him. No matter what he read in the guide book, whether he followed this advice or not was a decision he would have to make himself. A free man at last, the Colonel had a light breakfast, skipping his usual second cup of coffee, as what he planned to do was rent a room and go to bed. Nothing else struck him as both safe and sensible.

He had not slept well, but he never slept well on trains. It had been worse than usual, however, as it had dawned on the Colonel, as he lay in the berth, that his ticket to Chicago was something more than a coincidence. Was he fleeing from, or hurrying toward something? In the pocket of his coat he had two stubs, on the face of one was the name Kopfman, and on the face of the other Chicago. The Colonel was not a superstitious man, but the turn that his life had taken led him to mark the connection between apparently unrelated events. Several times, during the night, he heard the whistle blowing far down the tracks. For him? He was sure of it. He waited impatiently for the jolt to reach him in the caboose. He had still been waiting when he reached Chicago, where he spent half an hour he might have been sleeping looking for the name of Kopfman in the telephone directory. He found none, but neither did he feel relieved. He felt worse, as a matter of fact, as it seemed to increase his presentiment. Had he spelt the name wrong? Had there been something he had overlooked? Leaving the station he decided to walk, feeling safer in the street, in the open air, and he walked for half an hour before he found the right hotel. One without a bellhop, or the likelihood of chambermaids.

A wretched flight of stairs led him up from the street, where he rang a bell for the clerk, whom he followed down the hall to a room at the front. As they entered the room the warning bell on the drawbridge began to clang, and the shadow of the bridge moved like a hand across the yellow blinds. As the air was stale the clerk raised a window, and a cloud of dust puffed from the curtain. He leaned there a moment, gazing at the street, the lines of blocked traffic, the scow drifting on the river, and the Colonel remained at his back, near the center of the room. Had something stopped? Were they waiting for it to start up again? Above the warning bell, the idling motors, the Colonel thought he could hear the lapping of the water, just as he could smell, above the stench of the city, the river smell. As the shadow of the bridge moved on the blind the clerk left the room, leaving the key in the door, and the Colonel closed his eyes as if to shut out the blast of the horns. Like a pack of unleashed baying hounds, the traffic began to flow.

When the Colonel tried to lower the blind a piece came off in his hands, tearing like paper, and he turned from the window to face the calendar over the bed.

The Year of Our Lord

1 9 2 7

It gave the Colonel quite a start. Was it the year, or just that way of putting it? It seemed a long time ago, and that he, the Colonel, had stepped into a room where nothing had occurred, where time had stopped, so to speak, with the calendar. But the date seemed familiar. The word Lindbergh crossed the Colonel's mind. The young hero had certainly come to Chicago, perhaps he had passed beneath this very window, and if the window had been open the cheers would have entered the room. The nasal boos of Hyman Kopfman, the cheers of Paul Kopfman, a soldier of Christ. And then the window had been closed, and these sounds had been trapped. Were they still to be heard? The Colonel tipped his head back, lidded his eyes, and heard the drip-drip of water in the sink in the corner; from this quarter also he detected the familiar smell of urine. On the table was a book, a Gideon Bible, with a raw red stain on the leaves, and the Colonel picked it up, squinted his eyes to read—

And the children of Israel did evil in the sight of the Lord.

So they did, did they? Well, they were all of one company.

How long ago did they do it? Several thousand years ago, perhaps. But the trapped air in the room seemed to hold echoes of it. The same old story. The doing of evil in the sight of the Lord. The Colonel cocked his head, seeing in the flecked mirror the tired faded eyes of Colonel Foss, but feeling behind him, in the mirror itself, the eyes of the Lord. It did not disturb him. No, he felt less alone. Over the end of the bed he folded his coat, then he seated himself and removed his shoes, loosened the belt of his pants, and lay out on his back in the sight of the Lord.

Did he doze off? Perhaps, as something woke him up. He was aware of a vibration in the bed that never left the room. The springs on which he lay gave off a sound like a plucked harp. Over his head, like a clouded eye, a frosted bulb was suspended from the ceiling, and a knot had been looped in the cord to shorten it. He was able to observe that the cord was lumpy with flies. That the bulb sustained an even, somewhat elliptical swing. This movement did not trouble the flies, however, any more than the movement of the sun or the earth seemed to trouble the man lying on the bed. Perhaps he didn't like the way they accepted it. He raised his right arm, then let it fall with quite a thud on the bed frame, and this jolt was communicated to the dangling cord. How did he know? One of the flies on the cord dropped off. He dropped a foot or two, then he recovered, there was a droning sound as his motor started, and he flew head on, with a loud dry snap, into the yellow blind. From there he dropped to the floor, where he buzzed like a fly trapped in a bottle, and then quickly, like a toy,

89

he ran down. The bulb continued its elliptical movement, the twanging vibration returned to the springs, and the Colonel, closing his eyes, dropped off to sleep.

Then he was on his feet in the corner of the room. He stood facing the wall, and the knuckles of his hands were red and sore. He had been pounding on the wall as a cloud of dust hung in the light that streamed through the window. This disturbance had also unsettled the flies and the room seemed to be full of them. On his way back to the bed one of them flew into his face. He struck out at it wildly, bruising his hand on the iron frame of the bed, and as he stood there, waiting, the fly struck him again.

He took a towel from the rack, rolled it up firmly, then doubled it over so that it made a soft club. In the center of the room, his arms at his side, he played dead. He observed the movements of the flies through half lidded eyes. When he was struck again he flailed the air wildly: sweat ran into his eyes and glistened on the backs of his hands. The lightness of the towel, and the violence of his motions, had made his arm sore. He wet the towel at the sink, so he could swing it like a club. He came back to the center of the room again and stood there, his arm half cocked, his eyes half closed. He was ready, waiting, when the fly flew into his mouth. In and out, not more than an instant, but the buzzing sensation remained on his tongue, and the drone seemed to be trapped within his own head. He flailed the air, then he calmed himself. He let the towel hang and looped a hard knot at the end. Then he stalked the fly—there were others, but this one was larger, more distracted, and struck the yellow blinds with a sharp metallic ping. It was scared, this fly, and the Colonel could hear it in the sound of the motor, pitched too high, like the whine of a diving jet. He stalked it with all of his cunning, nursing his strength. He kept this fly on the move, he gave it no rest, and he prepared himself for the moment when he would step in, like a bull fighter, for the kill. It was not necessary, however, as the fly gave up. Without warning, without apparent reason, his motor went dead and he dropped to the bed within arm's reach of the Colonel, an easy target on the spread. Was he looking for mercy? Had he had enough? The Colonel took a fresh grip on the towel, measured his distance, then let the knot in the towel swing behind him for a full stroke.

Was it this movement he detected in the mirror? He saw this

figure with the legs spread, the arm upraised with the knot dangling, and he saw, he strained his eyes to see, the fly on the bed. Was it the light in the room, his overwrought imagination, or was it the stamp that the dream had left upon him? The figure in the mirror had the Colonel's body, but not his face. No, the face was new, and the luminous eyes gazed upon the bed where the fly, for no reason whatsoever, had rolled over on its back. There was no twitching of the legs, no movement of the wings, but the Colonel saw the shadow darken the mirror and felt the breath of air as the wing of madness brushed his face. The other flies flew around undisturbed, pinging on the blinds, buzzing in the curtains, and crawling unmolested on the Colonel's face and hands.

In the quiet the Colonel could hear the other flies, the happy ones, and he saw that two had returned to the lumpy light cord. Another came, then another, until, like homing pigeons, they were all back on the cord except for the fly that lay on the bed. This one he covered with the towel, then he dressed and left the room.

If there had been a telephone booth in the lobby the Colonel would have stepped in and called his wife, as he felt the need to hear a familiar voice. There was none, however, so he walked across the street to a drugstore, where he had a cup of coffee while waiting for a sailor to get out of the booth. The sailor wore a white suit, and he talked like a man who had the girl right there before him, but he seemed to be having trouble getting results. He dropped coin after coin into the slot. In his right hand he held the coins, and in his left several sheets of paper that the Colonel recognized as pages torn from the telephone book. Using his thumb nail as a marker, he checked off the numbers on his list. When he had run out of coins he left the booth and returned the sheaf of pages to the phone book, the tips sticking out as if to mark the place. The Colonel paused to see just what place this was and glance at the first torn page of the sailor's sheaf. It contained a listing of the Y.W.C.A.'s. That made the Colonel smile, that was amusing, but it also put him in mind of the Y.M.C.A.'s, which he found listed on the back of the page. The Colonel had a good head for certain names, and certain numbers, so he didn't have to take the sheet along with him: when he heard the buzzing signal he dialed the number carefully.

"Larrabee Y.M.C.A.—" said the voice, "good afternoon."

"Could I speak to Paul Kopfman?" the Colonel said.

"Paul who?"

"I am trying to get in touch—" the Colonel said, "with Paul Kopfman. I understand he was once with you."

"There's no one here by that name," said the voice. "There's nobody here by the name of Kopfman." When he pronounced the word Kopfman the Colonel heard a voice in the background. "Just a minute," said the clerk, "hold the wire for just a minute." Then he added, "Here is Mr. Hoppe."

"Hello—" said the Colonel.

"Paul—" said the voice, hoarsely, "is that you, Paul?"

"My name is Foss," said the Colonel, "and I'm trying to get in touch with Paul Kopfman."

There was no answer.

"Could you tell me where I might find him?" the Colonel said.

"Paul is missing—" said the voice.

The Colonel had his mouth open to speak when he realized what he had heard. "Missing—?" he repeated.

"Paul is missing," said the voice, and that was all. The Colonel waited, he heard the man cough.

"There's been a death in the family," the Colonel went on, "and I'm trying to get in touch with—"

"Who now—?" the voice interrupted.

"Hyman Kopfman," said the Colonel, thinking fast, "I'm an old friend of Hyman Kopfman."

"My God—" said the voice, nothing more.

"My name is Foss," said the Colonel, "and I was with Hyman Kopfman in his last illness." Still no answer. "Hello—?"

"Hyman Kopfman," said the voice. "Imagine that."

"We shared a room in the hospital," the Colonel said, "and when he passed on—"

"God bless him—"

"He often spoke of his brother Paul—"

"Paul is missing—" the voice interrupted, as if in answer to another question. It sounded like a refrain, a sentence that had been passed many times.

92

"I'm just passing through the city," the Colonel went on, "but I thought if Hyman Kopfman had any people—"

"Mr. Foss," said the voice, "would you find the time to stop and talk with me?"

"I only have an hour or two," the Colonel replied.

"My name is Hoppe," he said, "and this afternoon I'm afraid I'm on duty. I'm here at the Y. I'm afraid I can't get away from here."

"How far you out?" the Colonel said.

"If you're in the Loop," said Mr. Hoppe, "we're only about twenty minutes. Take a Clarke Street car, change at North Avenue."

"I'll see what I can do," the Colonel replied.

"Hyman Kopfman—you really knew him?" Mr. Hoppe sounded skeptical.

"We were together for several months," the Colonel said.

"Think of that," Mr. Hoppe said, with a good deal of feeling. "Think of that."

"I'll see what I can do," the Colonel repeated, and then he sat there, occupying the booth, until a woman came forward and rapped on the glass panel with her coin.

He rode north on a Clarke Street car, and though there were plenty of seats in the car he stood up front with his hands on the rail at the motorman's back. There he could see where he was going, a very important point. The Colonel was not indifferent to suffering, but as he saw neither hope nor moral in it, he avoided the spectacle of poverty whenever possible. The twenty minute ride through the slums left him depressed. The light reflected from the street troubled his eyes, and when he changed cars at North Avenue, he took two of the aspirin from the tin in the pocket of his coat. From the corner of North Avenue and Larrabee he could see, just beyond the elevated, the battered sign of the Y.M.C.A. The C had been knocked out of it. There appeared to be two entrances to the building, and the Colonel passed by the first one rather than disturb the group of boys who were playing craps. A small dark skinned boy rolled the dice against the soft stone of the steps, snapped his fingers, then leaned forward to scoop up, without comment, the coins.

The door to the second entrance was propped open with the butt of a billiard cue. Through the door blew a draft smelling of disinfectant and the chlorinated water of a swimming pool, and the Colonel could hear, as he stepped inside, the sound of a diving board vibrating. A short flight of steps led up to the lobby, and at the top of the stairs, just within the lobby doors, a tall, thin man stood twirling a long chain of keys. He stood with his back to the door, and the swinging keys, like the blades of a fan, blurred the face of the boy he was talking to.

"The ball is not my ball, Vito," the man said, and held the billiard ball out where the boy could see it, "the floor is not my floor or you could bounce the ball all you like." He paused there, then he said, "If it was my ball, you could have it, if it was my floor, you could bounce it, but it isn't my ball—it's the Y's ball." In the pause the swinging keys made a whirring sound, the boy made a grunt. "Now, you go think it over, Vito," he said, "and I'll keep the ball in the drawer here for you. When you remember whose ball it is, you come and ask me for it." Then he turned away, still swinging the keys, and looked at Colonel Foss who was standing on the first step from the bottom, a blank look on his face.

"You are Mr. Foss?" he asked.

"Why, yes—" said the Colonel.

"I'm Mr. Hoppe," said the tall man, and came down the steps to grasp the Colonel's hand and gaze directly into his eyes. Then he turned, as if the boy who had stepped to the lobby doors had spoken to him, or had rapped with the warped cue he held on the tile floor. "So you remember—?" he said, "Well, that's fine, Vito. I knew you would remember if you just thought it over." The boy said nothing. There was not the slightest movement of his head. "It's your ball, Vito—" Mr. Hoppe said, "you're free to play with it while Mr. Foss and I have a talk." Mr. Hoppe pressed the ball into the boy's dirty hand, and led him down the hall to his office at the back. One of the many keys on the chain opened it.

Mr. Hoppe appeared to be a man in his middle forties. His thinning wispy hair was grey, but in the privacy of his office his voice raised a notch, as if to indicate that he might be younger than he looked. That his graver voice, his sober side, was reserved for the smaller fry in the lobby. He crossed the room to open the blinds as the sun had left that side of the building, but it

94

was still bright on the buildings across the street. The angle was different, but the view was the same as the Colonel had enjoyed from the hospital, a close-up view of a crowded, bloody corner of the battlefield. Sitting down the Colonel took from his pocket a pack of cigarettes and waited for Mr. Hoppe to turn back from the window.

"You see that store, Mr. Foss?" The Colonel leaned forward to look in the direction Hoppe was pointing. He saw a small grocery store. Over the store the windows were crowded with plants. "He lived there awhile," Mr. Hoppe went on, "was living there when he disappeared."

"He just wandered off—?"

"Just disappeared—" said Hoppe, and turned from the window to shrug his shoulders, gaze at the palms of his hands.

"Smoke—?" said the Colonel, and held out the pack, but Mr. Hoppe slowly wagged his head.

"I'm a non-smoker, Mr. Foss." He smiled, then said, "You see, in my business—" and waved one hand toward the wall of his office, where several large Y.M.C.A. posters were displayed. They bore the legend—A Healthy Mind in a Sound Body—and featured several young athletes breaking the tape.

"It's a filthy habit," the Colonel said, and drew a cigarette from the pack, lit it. As he inhaled the smoke, his head seemed to clear.

"I don't seem to have an ash tray, Mr. Foss—" Hoppe said, and gazed around the room as if he might spot one, but the Colonel indicated that it was hardly necessary. He raised his hat, which he had placed on the floor, and dropped the ashes of the cigarette into the crown. This seemed to make quite an impression on Mr. Hoppe.

"There are a good many things to be said for the army," Mr. Hoppe said, seating himself behind his desk, "a good many things."

"Yes, I suppose there are," the Colonel replied. Nothing particular came to his mind as he sat there, gazing through the window, but Mr. Hoppe studying his face, seemed satisfied. "You say he just wandered off—" the Colonel repeated.

"One day he was here, the next day he was gone." From the pocket of his coat Mr. Hoppe took a mint, popped it into his mouth. As it dissolved he relaxed, and pushed his chair back

95

from the desk. A billiard ball raced across the floor of the lobby, struck the wall, then slowly rolled back, but Mr. Hoppe did not rise from the chair. "People often ask me," he said, "why I once put Paul's name in the phone book, as it's been—" he stopped to consider, "more than ten years." He paused there, until he saw that the Colonel had managed to form the question, then he added, "Say, you're lost. Say, you don't know who you are. In a case like that you just might look in the phone book—you might look yourself up." When the Colonel didn't question that he said, "My wife thinks I'm crazy—you think so?"

"I was just going to say," said the Colonel, "that I looked in the book myself."

"There you are," said Hoppe, "there you are, and what's to keep a man—once he gets the habit—from looking in the book for anything he thinks is lost?"

On the sole of his shoe, the Colonel stubbed his cigarette, split the paper with his thumbnail, dropped the loose tobacco into his hat.

"You don't think I'm crazy—?" Hoppe said, but it was not a question he put to the Colonel. His eyes were turned to the window: he was staring at the street where an ice wagon had drawn up to the curb. Under the wagon the sparrows had gathered, and there they congregated, in the cool, dripping shade, until the old mare at the front raised her frazzled tail and dropped them a feast. They did not move, not a bird, when she dragged the wagon off.

"What do you think was the trouble?" the Colonel asked, and watched a flock of pigeons chase off the sparrows, but Mr. Hoppe didn't seem to be listening. His gaze still out the window, he said, "As it turned out, it was quite a loss for me. Personal loss. He'd got to be my right hand man. Grew up in the work. I had him slated for something here."

The word slated, the Colonel decided, would have sounded strange in the lobby, but it sounded all right in Mr. Hoppe's private room.

"What do you think was the trouble?" the Colonel repeated.

"Trouble?" said Hoppe. "What do I think was the *trouble*?"

The Colonel gathered that he had used the wrong word. He couldn't think of a better one, however, but he saw that Mr. Hoppe was a different man when it crossed his mind that you

96

might be pulling his leg. "Hyman Kopfman didn't tell you, **Mr. Foss**?"

"We talked about many things," said the Colonel. "He had his own troubles. He lost a leg, then he lost an arm."

Mr. Hoppe put both hands to his face, and rubbed at his eyes. It was clear that that was not the trouble that he meant. He seemed to indicate that that was no trouble at all.

"He talked a lot about his people," the Colonel said, "but not much in the way of specific trouble—"

Mr. Hoppe pursed his lips. "Some things are difficult to talk about, Mr. Foss," he said.

"I suppose he talked more about Vienna than he did Chicago," said the Colonel, and he would have gone on, but Mr. Hoppe interrupted him.

"HA!" he said, as if the Colonel had made a cardinal point. It was something of a strange sound from Mr. Hoppe, and he winced as if the effort hurt him. It had come of itself, like a hiccup, and caught him by surprise. A curious mocking smile, that he seemed unaware of, remained on his lips.

"Chicago was quite a change—" the Colonel went on, "from the way they used to live in Vienna," and another sound, even stranger than the first, escaped from Mr. Hoppe's lips. A kind of sad raspberry. A soft, vulgar, despairing sound. Something he had heard out there in the lobby, perhaps. Through the window they could see the waves of heat that rose from the top of a parked sedan and made the scene ripple as if reflected in a stream. The awning over the delicatessen window seemed to blow in a draft. As if he felt the heat for the first time, Mr. Hoppe leaned forward and switched on the fan, which stirred the ashes in the crown of the Colonel's hat. Although he faced the Colonel, he didn't seem to notice this. The fan swung around in a wide arc, and while it faced away, blowing out the window, the Colonel lit another cigarette.

"I often wonder how you smoke in hot weather," Mr. Hoppe said. The Colonel took this comment as it was meant, impersonally.

"You just smoke—" the Colonel replied, as it seemed as good an answer as any.

"In the winter—" Mr. Hoppe said, "in the winter I can see it. Used to think I'd like it myself. But in the summer—" he turned up his hands and gazed at the palms. There was cue dust on one of his fingers and he rubbed it off.

"It gets to be a habit," the Colonel said, casually, as he would to a very young person, who might honestly wonder why some men behaved as they did. He was not flip. He understood the question was serious enough.

"I suppose you smoke for different reasons," Hoppe said, and the Colonel realized that this *you* included all men but Mr. Hoppe. He didn't know too much about men, perhaps. Only about boys.

"It's something you can do—" the Colonel went on, before he realized that Mr. Hoppe, a busy man with boys, never lacked for something to do. Into the crown of his hat, the Colonel flicked the ash from his cigarette. Although the fan stirred the air in the room, and as it swung in an arc left a silence between them, the Colonel felt at his ease, as if he sat there by himself.

"I suppose it's relaxing—" Mr. Hoppe said, still trying to plumb this mystery, and wondering if what he had read about it was true. The Colonel smoked, and watched the fan blow it around the room. He was amused by the peace of mind that he seemed to feel in such a strange situation, and wondered if it was due to the fact that he needed food. He had forgotten, he had been too preoccupied, to eat. His mind, thanks to the tobacco, seemed to be both at peace with itself and lucid, but curiously disembodied from the man who sat in the chair. Mr. Hoppe seemed to remark this himself. He had been thinking aloud without embarrassment. Now he opened a drawer of his desk, took out a tin cup of the collapsible type, and walked to a water cooler in the corner of the room. As he let the water run, he said, "Mr. Foss, can I bring you a drink?"

"No, thank you." The Colonel shook his head. Mr. Hoppe had a long drink himself. He then collapsed the cup and brought it back to his desk. There he stood and faced the fan for a moment, letting it flap his unbuttoned coat, then he took another lozenge from his pocket, slipped it into his mouth. Lidding his eyes, he said, "He was the nicest boy we ever had."

The Colonel cleared his thoat. "It must have been a shock, Mr. Hoppe, it must have been quite a shock," then he waited for Mr. Hoppe. "Quite a little shock," the Colonel repeated, and on the face of the man who looked at him he saw an expression that he recognized. Mr. Hoppe was waiting, waiting and listening, as if he had heard the whistle far down the tracks and he was waiting for the jolt, the jar, to reach the caboose. He placed the tips of his fingers on the corner of his desk. "If you think it was shock enough," said the Colonel, "to turn a man into a woman—maybe I can help you, maybe I can give you a lead." Mr. Hoppe did not move, and the expression on his face did not change. "I know a Mrs. Tabori," said the Colonel, but as he pronounced the words Mr. Hoppe moved along the side of the desk like a man who was blind. He felt himself around the corner, he let himself down into his chair. He pressed his hands to his face, his arms close to his body, like a person overcome with weeping, and as he took them away he seemed to see, cupped in the palms, the mask of his face. "I could be wrong," said the Colonel, "but if there were no girls in the family—" There he stopped, as Mr. Hoppe pushed up from his chair, crossed the room to the file, and removed a folder. He returned to his chair and placed the folder before him on the desk.

"If you can spare the time—" Mr. Hoppe said, and the Colonel signified that he could by leaning back in the chair, placing the crown of his hat in his lap. Mr. Hoppe had taken a newspaper clipping from the folder, sat reading it.

"Emil Tabori—" he said absently, "case of— He came over first. Mrs. Kopfman's older brother. He came over first, found a place for them to live." Mr. Hoppe paused. "At that time he was a man in his forties, worked in the freight yards near the sewage canal." He looked toward the window, in the direction of the freight yards. "He didn't learn much English, Mr. Foss, and living alone he didn't need it. He walked to work and back. He talked German with the other immigrants. He saved money, and everything he saved he sent to her. Found a place not far from here for them all to live."

"Amazing how these fellows get ahead," the Colonel said.

"Just before Christmas we had this blizzard. Snow piled up in the streets. On the day before Christmas he didn't get home, and he was still missing on New Year's. Paul spoke to me about it. I got in touch with the police. He never came home, or showed up at his work, and the police knew nothing about him." Mr. Hoppe paused there, then went on, "In April of that year the drifts of winter began to melt." He stopped and said, matter-of-factly, "I'm sure you know about such things, Mr. Foss—"

The Colonel was not sure. What things?

"When a dead man is found in the streets," said Mr. Hoppe, "someone has to pick him up, he has to be buried." The Colonel felt his head nodding. "Dead bodies are a problem, Mr. Foss, since it costs money to bury them. But they are also worth money. As you know, there are people looking for them."

"What's a good body worth?" the Colonel inquired.

Mr. Hoppe didn't seem to hear that. "There is the record of a sale," he continued, "of a body with the first joint missing, first finger, of the left hand. In the Kopfman family this missing joint was quite a joke. When Emil Tabori put that finger to his ear it appeared to have entered his head. Very amusing, of course." Colonel Foss looked at his own fingers, flexed the joints. "In May a medical student, who made such things a hobby, recognized the hand that he was dissecting. He put formaldehyde in his lunch pail and brought the hand to Mrs. Kopfman for identification. Paul was there at the time. He left the house in the evening and was not seen again."

The Colonel started to speak, but seemed to have a frog in his throat. He pushed up from the chair, glancing at his watch, but Mr. Hoppe remained at the window. What he saw led him to say, "There's a faith that moves mountains, Mr. Foss," as if he saw it before him, in operation. "Would such a faith find it hard to change the nature of man?"

It was hardly necessary for Colonel Foss to comment on that. Mr. Hoppe had crossed the room to open the door, and the two of them walked down the hall to the lobby, where a billiard ball was rolling across the floor. Mr. Hoppe let it roll, giving the boy a smile as he shook Colonel Foss' hand, his own eyes turned inward with Mrs. Tabori's luminous gaze.

100

10

In the Dearborn station the Colonel saw the name of Colorado Springs on a railroad poster, with Indians in the foreground and snow capped peaks that looked far away, far away. He bought a ticket to this place and sat in the club car, a tall drink in his hand, gazing absently at the prairie night, and the small prairie towns. He saw the bug spotted lights over the empty corners, he saw the houses were dark. As if there were no walls to these houses he saw the quilt frame in the room at the back and the sewing machine drawer full of newspaper clippings and sound advice. He saw the early photographs of big men like Milton Ashley, small men like himself. He was alone in the car when they crossed the Mississippi, the train lights blurred on the muddy water, and on the far side of the river, in Davenport, he got off. He stood on the platform, listening to the tolling engine bell. The porter in the club car leaned out the window to stare at him. When this train left he inquired in the station for the next train east, bought a ticket, and having set his watch an hour ahead somewhere, he set it back again. Across the street from the station was an all night diner where he had some eggs, several cups of coffee, and sat in a booth near the juke box, smoking, and waiting for his train.

Through the wide diner window, facing the east, he watched the new day come to Illinois, then cross the river, like a spreading fire, and come to Iowa. The blinking neon sign no longer

101

showed red on the walk. A sleepy girl took the place of the man behind the counter, and several local trucks with men who knew the girl, stopped by for coffee, conversation, and a stack of hot cakes. Coins were dropped into the juke box. A woman sang of fickle love. When he stepped into the street the Colonel could hear, like the rumble of guns north of the city, the rising whine of traffic on the industrial pike. At the entrance to the bridge the stop lights blinked on, a motorman clanged a lonely trolley bell, and a bundle of papers was thrown from the back of a newspaper truck. West of town, blowing east, the Colonel heard the whistle of his train, and the slack, slapping sound of the driving rods when the engine began to coast.

A milk train, making all the stops, the Colonel sat up front near the water cooler, where he could see, through the door, the baggage car rocking along the tracks. Later, the window was opened, and cinders and dust collected in his hair. When he ate a sandwich he could taste the grit between his teeth. Out of one town he was locked in the toilet, while the coach was switched around in the yards, but when the door was unlocked the conductor found him just sitting there. He took no offense, and was easily persuaded to find a better seat.

In Chicago he was changed to another train. Now and then he slept, with his hat tipped over his face. Nearing New York, as the train was crowded, he shared his seat with the conductor, and made civil answers when he was spoken to. Toward morning he slept, his mouth open, his head bobbing on a rented pillow, his uniform stained with what had leaked from a carton of milk. He woke up, his ears ringing, in the tunnel approaching New York. In the station he used the escalators, walked underground to the subway, then stood up with the crowd of theatre people on their way home. The elevator boy in the St. George station greeted him. In the street he faced the cool breeze off the river, with its minty toothpaste smell, blending with coffee when he turned and walked to the south. In front of the building where he lived a car was parked. As he drew alongside this car the Colonel could hear the dance music, and see the glow, behind the wheel, of a cigarette. As he went up the steps a voice spoke to him.

"Colonel Foss?" The Colonel stopped, turned on his heel, and saw the face of a boy in the lowered car window. He looked very young. "Colonel Foss?" he repeated, and the Colonel nodded his

102

head. "I'm Larry Oakley," the boy said, but when the Colonel's face did not light up, he added, "Mrs. Oakley's son. My mother is Mrs. Foss' old friend."

"Oh—" said the Colonel. "Oh, yes," and waited for the boy to go on. "How is your mother?" asked the Colonel, as the boy climbed out of the car. He was a tall, man-sized boy, an inch or two taller than the Colonel, and he seemed to be embarrassed to find the Colonel so small. He had probably heard what a big soldier he was.

"Colonel Foss—" he repeated. Something in the way he collected himself made the Colonel realize that whatever followed had been learned by heart. If it followed, since he seemed to have forgotten whatever it was.

"Mrs. Foss is over with your mother?" said the Colonel.

"Colonel Foss—" the boy began again, "it falls on me to tell you that Mrs. Foss has had a terrible accident."

The Colonel's first sensation was relief, as the boy had got it out. Then it occurred to him what he had said.

"An accident?"

"My mother would be here," said the boy, "but it was just too much of a shock. She was here when it happened. We were both here." Then he stepped back and waited for the shock to show in the Colonel's face.

"Mrs. Foss has had an accident?" said the Colonel. He felt nothing, absolutely nothing.

"Yesterday evening," said the boy, "we were both here, me and my mother, as Mrs. Foss had asked my mother to come and stay with her. You weren't here. I guess she didn't want to be alone."

"I was called out of town," the Colonel said.

"That's what she said, that's what she called and said. She asked my mother to come stay with her till you got back."

"There was an accident?" The Colonel turned to face the building. He looked up the front to the lighted window at the top.

"She fell," said the boy. "She fell off the balcony at the back."

The Colonel made an involuntary movement toward the railing at the side of the steps, grasped it firmly, then released it, as if it were hot.

103

"There's an awful low railing there," said the boy, "it's just no real railing at all." He wagged his head from side to side to think of it.

"Mrs. Foss is dead?" the Colonel asked.

"She still wasn't late this evening. She's just paralyzed. She can't move or talk." Then he seemed to remember that he had been told not to mention such terrible matters, to say instead something consoling, something that would help. "It's a terrible thing, Mr. Foss, but I guess it just couldn't be helped."

"You were there? You saw her fall?"

"We didn't really see her fall," said the boy, "we were in front, playing five hundred, and Mrs. Foss said excuse me, I just thought of something. Then she left the cards face down on the table and walked through to the back and we sat there, waiting. We waited quite awhile. When she didn't return my mother said to me that she was worried about Mrs. Foss, and this wasn't at all like her. She looked worried, as if there was something on her mind. Then my mother went back and opened the door—that's the one to the kitchen, and I could see on past her to where the doors were open at the back. They were wide open and I could see the lights across in New York. Right at that point my mother —"

"Young man," said the Colonel, interrupting, "do you have a match?"

"Why sure," said the boy, and the Colonel let him strike it, let him hold it in his cupped hands, and his own hands he returned to the pockets of his coat.

"I think I see how it happened—" the Colonel said, and let the smoke gather between them.

"She probably went back there," said the boy, "for a breath of fresh air, or something."

"I think I see the picture," the Colonel said.

"Mrs. Crowther, who was with us, stayed with my mother, and I went down because we had to make sure—" the boy shook his head. "It's four stories. That's a long drop."

The Colonel stepped into the dim light of the vestibule, facing the mail boxes. The key to the mail box was still in his coat— in the small coin pocket he reserved for keys—and he opened the box, saw that it was empty, closed it again. The boy remained on the steps outside, watching him. The Colonel realized that he

104

had been told to keep an eye on the Colonel, see how he took it, as something like this might be too much of a shock. He should hang around and see how things went off. If anything happened, why, he should step forward and offer to help. The Colonel turned to look at the boy again, his awkward frame, his wide young shoulders, and he said, "Young man, I think I forgot my key."

"You like me to ring for you, sir?" the boy said, as if that might be quite a little problem. He came to stand beside the Colonel, look at the row of faded names.

"Mrs. Tabori," the Colonel asked, pronouncing the name carefully, "is still upstairs?"

"You mean the maid?" The Colonel nodded. "Oh sure," he said, and then as if in explanation, "she slept through it all. She doesn't even know it happened." He shook his head at the strange ironies of life. "Besides—" he said, looking at the Colonel's face, "isn't she deaf?"

"Mrs. Tabori is a little hard of hearing."

"You think she'll hear it if I ring?"

"We can try," the Colonel said, and as the boy pressed on the button, he turned to face the door, his eyes on the knob.

"She's probably in bed now," said the boy, and gave the button another push. As he did, the Colonel heard the voice in the speaking tube.

"Hello—?" it said.

"This is Colonel Foss," said the boy, "would you please buzz the door?"

"AHHhhhh—" came the reply, and a moment later the door buzzed loudly. The young man stepped around the Colonel and opened it.

"Young man," the Colonel said, "I seem to be very tired, and there is no lift in this building."

"I'd be glad to," said the boy, and put a firm hand under his arm. As the door closed behind them, he said, "Mother said I should tell you that she knows how it is. She—we lost father, you know." Then he paused and said, "But father died in bed. It was nothing like this."

On the third floor landing the Colonel paused, as he was breathing heavily, and wiped his face with a napkin he had been given on the train. The boy stood to one side, prepared to catch him when he dropped. He was a child, the Colonel realized, disguised as a man, his mind neatly fitted with the answers to the problems that might turn up. But it helped, nevertheless, to have him along. The Colonel put a hand on his shoulder and said, "You were sitting down there waiting for me?"

"Just tonight," said the boy, "last night we had a league ball game."

"How did it come out?" the Colonel said.

"We won—" said the boy, "we—" then he suddenly remembered the occasion. "Mother figured you wouldn't be gone more than a day or two."

"As it happens, I'm back a day early," the Colonel said.

"Mother figured on that," said the boy, "she says you can sense a personal tragedy. She says you can sense it like birds know their way back."

"I think that's possible," the Colonel replied.

"Maybe all you feel is that something is wrong, but if you feel it strong enough you turn around and come back. Is that what you felt?" The Colonel put out his hand to the bannister. Perhaps it showed in his face, for the boy said, "Whoops—Mr. Foss, now you take it easy," and took the Colonel's arm again. In this manner they went up the last flight of stairs. At the top Mrs. Tabori was there to greet them, wearing one of his wife's shortened bathrobes, but on her head, drawn down for the night, her own tasseled nightcap.

"Good evening—" the Colonel said, and for a moment the creature fixed him with her eyes, luminous as ever, gazing on him with tenderness.

"AHHHhhhhh—" she said, and as her head was wagging the sound came forth like a musical note, the echo vibrating after she had left the hall. As he stepped to the door the Colonel saw that the Simmons day-bed had been prepared, the pillow puffed, and the covers turned back as usual.

"You see—" said the boy, in a hushed voice, "You see, she doesn't know anything's happened," and he watched Mrs. Tabori, her tassel bobbing, go back through the apartment to the refrigerator door, where the cats, mewing, waited for her. She scooped them up, one in each arm, and disappeared into the back.

"You'd probably like something to drink," the Colonel said, as he hung up his coat in the closet, then turned to look at the boy's face. He saw that he would, but he had better breeding than to ask. "I think there's some beer—" the Colonel went on, and wondered if his mother would think that proper. "I'm pretty sure there's some ginger ale and Seven Up."

"I think I'd like beer," the boy said, "if you don't mind."

"Not at all, not at all—" the Colonel replied, but as he started toward the back he felt the cool river breeze blowing through the apartment. He took two or three steps then stopped: he could see the French doors at the back were open, the curtain flapping in the strong cross draft.

"Why, those doors are still open," said the boy, and he pushed by him, walked on ahead. He was half way across the room at the back when the Colonel made a sound as if he had been struck in the chest. It was not speech, merely a noise that had been forced out of him. The boy turned, and the Colonel said, "Oh, son—"

"Yes sir?"

"We like it open, son. We like it open at night for the draft."

"I suppose that's right." He nodded his head at the logic of it, then added, "But after what—"

"See if you can see a beer in there," the Colonel said, and leaned back from the refrigerator as if his own eyes were bad. The boy put in his head. "There's a quart, sir, there's a quart bottle." He turned to face the Colonel. "You think we ought to open a quart?"

"I think we can risk it," the Colonel replied, and the boy reached in for the bottle.

"It keeps me awake, but when I'm thirsty I sure like it."

The Colonel took the bottle opener from the hook over the sink, and from the shelf overhead two tall beer glasses. As he poured the beer he said, "I hope it puts me to sleep."

"You look pretty tired, you're probably all worn out."

The Colonel agreed. He had not slept for several nights. He was not accustomed, however, to any interest being shown in his condition, sympathetic interest, especially. He raised the glass and closed his eyes as he swallowed the beer.

"You really looked bushed," said the boy, and though the term was new to the Colonel, an army man, he understood it well enough. It was not every man, the boy's voice told him, that could really looked bushed.

"Yes, I guess I'm pretty pooped," the Colonel said, showing

he understood this kind of language, and he let himself down on the stool near the sink. He could feel the beer suds drying on his upper lip. The boy took the salt cellar from the table and sprinkled the head on his beer with salt, took two deep swallows, then belched before he could lower the glass. It made his eyes water, and he said, "I beg your pardon, sir—"

"That's nothing," said the Colonel, "first swallow or two is apt to do that."

"Knowing it's going to do it doesn't seem to help," the boy said. He had another swallow, which went down all right, then he said, "I don't want to be keeping you up, sir."

"Son—" said the Colonel, and wondered if the boy found a term like that affected, "it's getting pretty late. Why don't you just spend the night here?" He waved his hand from the front to the back of the apartment. "Plenty of beds, plenty of room."

"Mother said I should leave that up to you," the boy said.

The Colonel turned and said, "Here kitty-kitty-kitty—" not because he really wanted to see the cats, but in order to indicate in what a normal frame of mind he was. He was not suffering from shock. He was just an old man pretty well bushed. "Be glad to have you, son," he said, and when the cat, Jackson, brushed against his leg, he put down his hand and stroked the arching back, the upright tail.

"I see you like cats," the boy said, in a way that made it clear that he did not. "I like kittens all right," he went on, "but not cats."

The Colonel's eyes were wide, but now he closed them. "Each to his own nature, son—"

"That's the trouble," said the boy, "I don't like the nature of cats."

"What is the nature of cats?"

"You can care for them all right," said the boy, "but they don't seem to care for you." It was clear that he had read this somewhere, and it pleased him to be able to quote it. "He'd just as soon rub my leg as yours, and I don't even *like* him."

"I guess you're right," said the Colonel, "I guess that's the nature of cats." The boy's face revealed that he had spoken the truth, but perhaps he hadn't been so very tactful. At a time like this, shouldn't he let the old man have his cats?

"Mother tells me that the truth isn't nearly so important as

108

I like to think it is," he said.

"Sometimes it's hard to tell," said the Colonel, "what the truth is."

"That's what I like about Science," he said, "there you can demonstrate. If you can't demonstrate it all boils down to just your point of view." He took another swallow of his beer, and over the rim of his glasses he tried to figure out what the Colonel made of talk like that. Should he be talking so straight to an old man who was bushed? Would it lead him to walk out on the balcony and fall off himself?

The Colonel turned his gaze to the front and said, "Son, what plans do you have for changing the world?"

"You mean like Hitler, or you mean really change it?"

"I mean really change it."

The boy took a manly swig of the beer, wiped his mouth. "That's where we're probably different, Colonel Foss. I guess my generation has just seen too much."

The Colonel put his hand to the cat, stroked the long tail.

"If you can't change the world," the Colonel said, "what changes do you look forward to making?" On the boy's face, the lacy suds of beer drying with a bubbling sound on his lip, the Colonel saw an expression that he knew to be a familiar one. One that he reserved for his mother, perhaps, as a rule. A bemused concern, a mixture of pity and tenderness. As if the man before him, with his professional air, was dressed in some antique warrior's costume, but fancied himself, like Rip van Winkle, more or less up to date. The boy gazed upon him as the Colonel often gazed at the words engraved upon monuments, in wonder and amazement that men had once believed in such things. "We've got to change something, son—" he went on, but the boy smiled sadly, then said, "It's the same old stuff, Colonel Foss."

"You don't think it can be done?" the Colonel said. The boy shook his head. "What if you saw it?"

"What do you mean?" said the boy.

"What if you saw some changes made? If you saw it, would you believe it?"

"Seeing is believing," the boy replied. "You mean real changes?"

The Colonel lowered his eyes to the cat. He stroked the cat's back. "Real changes—like a change of nature."

109

"Like a dog into a cat?"

"Like that," the Colonel said.

The boy clucked his tongue. "That would be quite a change, wouldn't it?" The Colonel nodded his head, and the boy gazed at him, trying to determine if he was now a man of sane mind, or not. If the shock had seriously unsettled him.

"If I'm going to stay, Colonel Foss, maybe I better call Mother." He put his glass of beer on the table, looked around for the phone. It sat on a small end table in the front room.

"The phone is in here, son—" the Colonel said, and took his own glass of beer along with him, the cat following, and crossed the dining room. The phone itself was concealed by a hood, a snood Mrs. Foss called it, as she was of the opinion that the object itself was not decorative. As he removed this hood the Colonel noticed a small brass object—a bronze kitten—resting on the telephone pad. The Colonel had seen this kitten before, and as he raised it from the pad he remembered where—it had been part of Mrs. Tabori's menagerie. It had been going up the gang plank with a mouse, to board the ark. Now it served as a paper weight to hold the loose sheet beneath it on the table, and on this sheet, in his wife's firm hand,

SHOCKING DISCOVERY. COME HOME IMMEDIATELEY.

The Colonel read these words, lidded his eyes, then placed the bronze kitten back on top of them.

The boy dialed the number. The Colonel stood there, holding his beer, and heard the boy say Hello Mother? and then heard his mother say that if the Colonel was all right, she wanted him to come home. The boy couldn't answer that very well, so he turned from the phone and said, "Colonel Foss, Mother would like me to come home, if it's all right with you."

Was it the building, or his legs, that the Colonel felt trembling?

"Why, sure, son—" he said, "you run right along."

"He says it's all right, Mother," said the boy, "so I'll be right home." The Colonel heard his mother warn him to be careful, and to be sure and tell Colonel Foss that Mrs. Foss was in the same hospital where he once was.

"Mrs. Foss is now where you were," said the boy, then he put the phone down and took a step toward the Colonel, as he had dropped down, suddenly, on the bed. The beer rocked in his glass, but did not spill. "Why don't you just take it easy," the boy said, "why don't you just lay back and take it easy," and he took the beer glass from the Colonel's trembling hand. He carried the glass back to the kitchen, put it in the sink, then said, "I'm going to turn this light off, sir—" and tripped the switch on the wall. He came back to the front, and as he found the Colonel still sitting there, propped on his knees, he put a hand gently on the Colonel's shoulder and pushed him back. The Colonel tipped over easily enough. He lay out on his back, gazing at the arc the night light made on the ceiling, and the boy said, "Why don't you just let me take off your shoes?" He could think of no reason, so he said nothing, closed his eyes. The boy took off the shoes, and moved his feet as if they were separate from his body. "There—" he said, "now you just take it easy, you're really bushed." The Colonel agreed, he wagged his head up and down. "I'm going to turn off this light too," said the boy, and turned it off, so that he didn't see the Colonel's mouth drop open, or his right arm, like a man who was drowning, reach into the air. "Well, good night, Colonel Foss," the boy said, and as the hall door opened the Colonel's right arm, still in the air, dropped down on his face to block off the light.

"Good night, son—" he replied, and the boy was gone, the door was shut, and the Colonel was alone in the whispering night. He heard the boy race the motor, shift the gears, and the tires go whining down the street. On the ceiling, glowing faintly, the color changed from red to green. In the refrigerator several bottles tinkled together, then the motor clicked off and it was quiet. Very quiet. When the Colonel moved his head a finger seemed to pluck the day-bed springs. The boy had left the hood off the phone and the Colonel could see the numbers on the dial, and beside the telephone the bronze kitten on the white pad. Had she purloined the kitten? Had she gone into the room and picked it out? Had she been surprised, had she discovered the truth, and then come to the phone, the kitten still in her hand, to write out a telegram that she had never sent? He would never know, he was sure of that, and hearing a saucer rock in the kitchen he raised on his elbow and stared into the dark. At the door to the kitchen were the luminous eyes of a cat. They glowed in the darkness and seemed large for the eyes of a cat.

111

"Kitty, kitty, kitty—" the Colonel murmured, but the cat did not move. The eyes were like windows across the river, they did not blink. "Kitty, kitty—" the Colonel repeated, as they seemed to be getting larger. Were they coming toward him? There was no sound from the cat. "Kitty—" he said, and as figures are caught in a sculptured frieze, or a sudden disaster, this word remained on the Colonel's parted lips. He did not move, for a period of time he did not breathe. As men trapped in a flow of lava sometimes have an air of immortal ease, the Colonel lost, in this instant, his customary mortality. There was no way to tell what he had on his mind, but the expression on his face seemed to indicate that the loss had come to him in his sleep, in the shape of a dream.

Alone with Mrs. Tabori he surrendered to a remarkably soothing apprehension, so nameless yet so pervasive he felt it must be similar to the drug experience. He felt *high*. Euphoric might be the word. It was not a sensation he had previously experienced, and yet he had considerable knowledge of it. He had shared it with a creature who had known it well. Night after night, poor suffering Hyman Kopfman had turned his burning eyes on the Colonel, believing that fortunate unafflicted man to be asleep. He had not been, however, and for a tormented moment the Colonel had shared his doomed condition—as if the blood that flowed in Hyman Kopfman's veins flowed in his own. He had described this affliction as America! A curious and fevered hallucination, of course, but at those moments of drugged release he felt superior to whatever it was that was killing him. More than that, he felt transformed by it, an illusion common to many known to be hopeless. With each loss of part of himself he felt free of a tie that bound him. So did the Colonel— at this euphoric moment—and he did not stir when Mrs. Tabori, her skirts rustling, came to the door with the cat, Georgia, relaxed in her arms.

Had the Colonel called?

Who would know better than her? Perhaps he had. What, if anything, did he any longer have to fear? The bellhop was gone, and the Colonel's wife, if not gone, might be described as silenced, and he now alone shared with Mrs. Tabori an experience that would go unmentioned, its only traces being that it left them both remarkably free. It would appear that if the circumstances

112

were right, creatures of a miraculous aspect might be seen board-
ing the ark. Odd couples, signifying change for better or worse.

*Printed January 1972 in Santa Barbara for
the Black Sparrow Press by Noel Young. Design
by Barbara Martin. This edition is limited to
1500 copies in paper wrappers; 300 hardcover
copies numbered & signed by the author; & 26
copies handbound in boards by Earle Gray
lettered & signed by the author.*

Wright Morris

136